JESSICA BECK

THE DONUT MYSTERIES, BOOK 26
PUMPKIN PLEAS

The First Time Ever Published!

The 26th Donut Mystery.

Jessica Beck is the *New York Times* Bestselling Author of the Donut Mysteries, the Classic Diner Mysteries, the Ghost Cat Cozy Mysteries, and the Cast Iron Cooking Mysteries.

In no specific order, for Celeste Fenno, Pam Meadows, Jeff Biddle, Bev Ratliff, Hiemie Gandee, Scott Mease, Terry Murphy, David and Polly Perkins, Jamie Siebold, and most of all, Patty Hurley, for making my Carbide camp years some of my very best!

When newspaper owner Ray Blake goes missing, it's just the start of troubles for some of the people closest to donutmaker Suzanne Hart. Soon after, old flame Tom Thorndike is found dead at the bottom of a nearby waterfall. Was it foul play or simply a daredevil stunt gone wrong? Little does Suzanne know that her past is about to play a major role in her present, as well as her potentially perilous future.

CHAPTER 1

I WAS AWAKE AND WORKING LONG before anyone with any sense should be, making donuts for my customers at Donut Hearts, the small shop I owned and ran in April Springs, North Carolina. For the first part of every morning, I worked alone. It usually wasn't until I started frying the first cake donuts for the day that my assistant, Emma Blake, normally came in. Whenever I was at the donut shop, which was now down to five days a week, Emma did the dishes and kept up with a myriad of other chores for me while I handled the two main tasks at hand, producing the delightful treats we offered to the public and then working the counter out front selling them. On the two days a week I took off, Emma and her mother, Sharon, ran the place in my stead. On those days, Emma took over my duties, and Sharon handled her daughter's normal responsibilities. Though I'd known her for years, for some odd reason, I had a difficult time remembering the poor woman's name. She handled it with grace whenever I called her by the wrong moniker, but it seemed the harder I tried to get her name right, the worse I did.

As I dropped the first set of battered rounds into the hot oil, I glanced at the clock. Where was my assistant? Was it possible that I was ahead of schedule? No, my work was progressing at its usual pace.

So where was Emma? I started to worry as I continued dropping round after round into the hot oil, and by the time the cake donuts were iced and glazed, completing the first phase of my business, I was starting to get concerned. I had one more job to do before my break, and as I prepped the beginnings of the fresh dough for the yeast donuts, I decided that if Emma didn't show up by the time I finished, I was going to call her to see if she'd just overslept or if it was something more dire.

I had just finished assembling the ingredients for the yeast donuts when Emma finally walked in, looking decidedly upset about something.

"What's wrong? Did you oversleep?" I asked her as I studied her dire expression.

"I wish that was all that it was," Emma said as she rubbed her eyes. Had she been crying? "Suzanne, I haven't even been to bed yet. I'm afraid that it's really bad."

"Talk to me," I said as I hurried to finish the first steps of creating the yeast donuts, always the second phase of my operation. After I mixed everything together thoroughly, including the liquid, it was time to let the dough rest before I could move on to the next step. As soon as I removed the dough hook and covered the big mixing bowl with plastic wrap, I had time to give her my full attention.

"Dad never came home last night," Emma said worriedly. "Mom has been going crazy, and I've been doing my best to calm her down, but I'm starting to get worried myself. This isn't like him."

Emma's father, Ray Blake, owned and ran our local newspaper, *The April Springs Sentinel.* In many small towns, the publisher might be satisfied with running a few human-interest stories while selling enough ads to justify continuing the costs associated with printing their papers, but not Ray. He had it wedged deep in his mind that he was going to be a real newshound and scoop the larger papers around us someday, and he never rested in searching for that perfect story that would catapult him to the top.

So far, he hadn't found it, or anything even close, but that didn't keep him from looking.

"Where do you think he could be?" I asked her.

"I have no idea. At first I thought he might be at the newspaper; after all, he's been known to fall asleep at his desk in the past. But when he wouldn't answer any of our calls, I drove over there to check on him in person. There was no sign of him anywhere, Suzanne. Mom was really starting to get frantic, so I called Chief Grant. He and his night-shift cops have been out looking for Dad ever since, but they haven't had any luck, at least not so far."

"Could he be off somewhere chasing a story?" I asked as I put the dough hook in the sink with the rest of the dirty dishes I'd generated so far.

"It makes perfect sense if that's what he's doing, but why isn't he answering his phone?"

"Maybe he turned the ringer off," I suggested.

"No way. Dad would be too afraid of missing a big story to ever do that," Emma said. "I'm really worried about him, Suzanne."

"I completely understand," I said as I reached for my cell phone.

"Who are you calling?" she asked me.

"I'm waking Jake up," I said. "He can help get to the bottom of this." There was no doubt in my mind that my husband was sound asleep, but I knew that he wouldn't begrudge me the call, especially if it was for Emma's sake. He had a soft spot in his heart for my assistant, and everyone in town knew it.

"You don't have to do that," Emma said, putting her hand on mine.

"Nonsense. We need to find your father, and my husband is the perfect man for the job." It wasn't just wifely pride speaking, either. Jake Bishop had served with distinction with the state police, rising all the way to investigator before leaving the force in order to spend more time with me. He'd temporarily taken over the reins as the leader for our local police force, but after turning things over to his second in command, Jake was back in civilian life again.

"Are you sure he won't be upset about you calling him in the middle of the night?" Emma asked me.

"It'll be fine." I finished dialing my husband's cell phone number, and to my surprise, he answered on the first ring. What's more, he sounded wide awake.

"Hey, Suzanne, what's up?"

"You don't sound a bit sleepy," I said, almost as though I were blaming him for being awake.

"Sharon called me twenty minutes ago. She's worried about Ray, so I told her I'd help her look for him. I was just about to call you, but I'm guessing that Emma's already told you the news. It's no secret that I'm not the man's biggest fan, but I happen to like the women in his life, so I agreed to help out any way that I could."

"I'm glad. Jake, should I shut the donut shop down so we can both help with the search?" I asked.

After a slight hesitation, he said, "I wouldn't if I were you. I believe Sharon's mobilized the entire town, and they're going to be hungry come sunup. I've got a feeling that your donuts are going to be greatly appreciated by one and all."

"That makes sense," I said. "You make a good point, but I can handle things here by myself. Emma is going to want to be with her mother, so as soon as we get off the phone, I'm sending her on her way."

I looked over and saw my assistant nodding her thanks and reaching for her jacket. It was October, and the mornings were getting a distinct chill in the air the closer we got to Halloween.

"That's the spirit," he said. "I'll keep in touch, unless you want me to come by and lend you a hand at the shop."

"As much as I appreciate the offer, I think I'll be fine on my own." After all, I ran the place by myself one day a week anyway, so it wouldn't be that much of a hardship. Besides, Emma needed to be out looking for her dad alongside her mother. In his defense, Jake had tried to help me out at the shop a few times in the past, but I'd spent more time explaining and demonstrating what I'd wanted him to do than the tasks would have taken me to simply perform myself.

"Let me know if you change your mind," he said, the relief clear in his voice, and then we hung up.

"Suzanne, I really can stay if you need me here," Emma offered.

"Nonsense. Go be with your mother. I can handle things at the donut shop just fine on my own."

"Thanks, Suzanne. You're the best," she said as she hugged me.

"Try not to worry. I'm sure your father is fine," I said as I gave her back a few quick pats of consolation.

"I hope so," Emma said, and then she was gone.

Suddenly, my break was over. Now I had dishes to do, and then I had to get going on those yeast donuts. There was a reason Emma worked at Donut Hearts with me, and it wasn't just to keep me company. While I could do a fairly decent job of handling everything myself, it was exhausting, but it sounded as though a great many people in town were making sacrifices of their own searching for the missing newshound, so I could do my share, too.

Running hot water into the large sink, I started cleaning up the pots, pans, and utensils I'd used earlier, and I began to plot out the rest of my morning now that I knew I would be soloing at Donut Hearts. Ray's disappearance soon faded into the background of my thoughts as I got busy with my chores, but it never completely left my mind. Where could the man possibly be? If he was off chasing a story, why hadn't he at least told his family what he was up to? I had a feeling that if he was found alive and well, he was going to get the reprimand of his life from his wife and daughter for worrying them needlessly.

At least I hoped that was how the story ended.

The other possibility was too grim to even consider. I couldn't imagine how it would impact Emma and her mother if something had happened to Ray. It would be a blow that would be tough to recover from, and speaking as someone who had experienced losses in her own life, I wouldn't wish that on anyone.

CHAPTER 2

I T WAS A GREAT DEAL of work making the donuts by myself, keeping the kitchen clean, and then waiting on customers once I opened my shop for business. I suspected that I'd be there until well past noon washing dishes, and that was if I was lucky, but it was a sacrifice I was willing to make. By the time I was ready to greet the public and start selling donuts at six a.m., I was desperately in need of a real break, but I wasn't going to get one for hours yet. I loved what I did for a living, but sometimes it could be a bit much, even though I still wouldn't trade places with anyone in the world.

When the mayor of April Springs—and my dear friend— George Morris walked in, I realized one of the reasons I was so happy to have my life. Besides earning me a precarious income, my shop afforded me the opportunity to stay in close touch with many of my friends and family in the area. After all, just about everyone I knew loved donuts. They were frequent visitors to my shop, and I was more than happy to cater to every whim, and every sweet tooth, too.

"Not that I'm not happy to see you, but why aren't you out looking with the rest of the town? I figured you'd be leading a search party of your own," I told the mayor.

"Search party? What happened? Who's missing?" It was pretty obvious that he hadn't heard the latest news.

"Nobody told you? Ray Blake has vanished off the face of the earth."

7

"No, he hasn't," George said with a puzzled expression.

"He surely has. Most of April Springs has been out looking for him since four a.m. He didn't come home last night, and Emma and Sharon are frantic with worry."

George frowned. "That's odd."

"You're telling me. They're scared to death that something has happened to him."

"That's not what I meant," the mayor said. "Ray called me yesterday around six, and everything seemed fine with him then. I wonder what happened to him in the meantime?"

"Why was the newspaper man calling you?" I asked the mayor.

"I'm an important man in this town, young lady. Why shouldn't he call me?" George asked with a shrug. Was he really going to try to duck my question? If he thought I was just going to let it go, he'd seriously underestimated my determination to find out what was going on.

"I didn't mean to imply that you weren't," I said levelly. "I'm just wondering what he was calling you about. Do you mind telling me what he wanted, or was it confidential?"

"If it was, Ray didn't warn me to keep it to myself." The mayor sighed heavily, and then he looked at me for a moment before he spoke again. "You're not going to give this up until you find out what we talked about, are you?"

"Do you even have to ask me that question?" I posed with a grin.

"No, not really. If you must know, he was asking me something about Tom Thorndike."

"Tommy? What did he want to know about him?" Tommy, or Tom as he liked to be called now, had been my boyfriend all through the sixth grade, but we'd parted ways when Cindy Bottoms had suddenly, and almost miraculously, developed overnight. Tommy lost all interest in me at that point, and I'd been crushed for nearly two weeks, that is until Clark Davis started sitting with me at lunch, something that Grace Gauge, my best friend then and now, never let me forget to this day. Clark had gotten married straight out of high school, and now he had enough children to form his own coed basketball team. As for Tommy, we'd dated again for a few months in high school, but he'd gotten too attached, and I'd broken up with him because of his neediness. He'd disappeared for a while just before we were all set to graduate, only to reappear a few months ago. Tom kept very quiet about what he'd been up to in the intervening years, and frankly, I hadn't been curious enough about him to try to find out where he'd been or why he'd come back to town all these years later.

"Suzanne, I don't know if you've heard any of the rumors, but evidently Tom recently came into a great deal of money."

"He didn't inherit it, did he?" I asked. I'd known the Thorndikes forever, but I didn't realize anyone in the family had any serious money.

"I have no idea, and frankly, it's no one's business where it came from. Suzanne, you know how Ray operates. He got some wild theory about where the money came from based on nothing but his overactive imagination, and he started digging around when he found out that Tom bought a brand-new truck with cash last week."

"I can understand how Ray got excited about that, but where exactly do you fit into the picture?" I asked George.

"I'm not sure if I should tell you that part or not," the mayor said, suddenly looking uncomfortable about my question.

"Why not? Did Tom make you pledge an oath of secrecy about something?" I asked, half joking.

George frowned for a moment, and then he shook his head. "I suppose it's going to get out soon enough now that Ray is digging into it. Do me a favor and don't tell anyone that I'm the one who told you, would you?"

"I won't say a word about your involvement." I was really starting to get intrigued now.

"The reason Tom and I have been close over the years, and the reason Ray asked me about him, is because I arrested him when he was a senior in high school," George said with a sigh.

"You *arrested* him? What did he do? Is that why he disappeared all of a sudden?" My questions came out in a rush. This was a side of Tom Thorndike I hadn't expected.

"One night he asked his mother if he could borrow her car, and evidently they had a fight when she said no. I don't know if you remember, but Tom had quite a temper back then. He grabbed the keys anyway, and she called us to report that her car had been stolen. I was on the police force back then, and I happened to catch the call."

"Did you actually arrest him for stealing his own mother's car?" I asked. I knew George could be strict at times, but that sounded a little harsh to me.

"If that was all there'd been to it, I would have done my best to talk her out of it, but the car needed gas, and Tom didn't have any money. He was in the process of holding up a gas station out on the highway when I found him, and that was something I couldn't overlook."

"Was he actually armed?" I asked, incredulous that the boy I'd known had done something so reckless.

"No, but you know he's always been big and muscular. He threatened the clerk with a beating, and the kid behind the counter wasn't going to take the chance that he might not be bluffing. Tom was leaving the building as I was going in. He didn't put up a fight, but I still had no choice. I had to arrest him."

"I'm shocked to hear all of this so many years later," I said, fascinated that I'd never heard this story before. That was the way with small towns sometimes. The most innocuous things spread like wildfire, while a legitimate story got buried in the weeds.

"The courts were backed up here, so the case was tried in Union Square. I testified on Tom's behalf, and the judge took it into consideration. His mother was furious with me. She wanted her boy taught a lesson; she was a real piece of work. He still had to do jail time, but Tom and I kept in touch. Prison wasn't an easy place for him to be, and he kept getting himself into trouble with that temper of his. By the time he got out, we were friends. Then he vanished, and I didn't hear another word from him until he came back into town a few months ago."

"Does that mean that you honestly don't know where he got the money?" I asked.

"Like I said before, I don't have a clue."

"But you suspect something, don't you?" He did; I could see it in his eyes.

"Suzanne, he was a kid who did something stupid once, and he compounded his mistake with an overactive temper. That didn't make him a bad person then, or now, for that matter. He paid his debt to society, so as far as I'm concerned, he's square with society."

This was the George I knew and loved, gruff on the exterior, but caring and compassionate underneath, though he would have denied possessing those traits with his dying breath.

"I'm curious about something. How did Ray find out about your connection to Tom?" I asked him.

"I'm not sure. Maybe he found out about Tom's past. If he did, and he started digging, I'm betting that he saw the visitor's log at the prison. My name was written there four times a year for every year Tom served."

A sudden thought chilled me. "George, do you think Tom could be involved with Ray's disappearance?"

Inside

"No. I don't believe that for a second." It was clear that I'd pushed him a little too far, but I couldn't back off yet.

"You said it yourself, though. He had a temper back then," I reminded him. "There's no reason to assume that he still doesn't. If Ray pushed him too hard, is it that hard to imagine him pushing back?"

"He's a grown man, Suzanne. People can change, or don't you believe that?"

"As a general rule, I'd have to say no, I don't, but I realize that there are exceptions." Max, my ex-husband, was one such example. He'd been a womanizer even during our marriage, but since he'd started dating my friend Emily Hargraves, he hadn't strayed once, at least as far as I knew. There were a few other folks I knew who had also proved that they could change, but mostly, old habits and ways seemed to die hard in folks.

"Well, he's *one* of the exceptions, at least in my book," George said. "I'd better go see if I can find him before this thing gets out of hand."

"I'd say it's a little too late for that," I said as George started to walk out of the donut shop empty-handed.

"Hey, you forgot your donut," I reminded him.

"Thanks, but I suddenly lost my appetite," the mayor said.

"You still need to eat," I said as I bagged an old-fashioned donut for him and grabbed a paper cup. As I added coffee to it, George offered me money. I just shook my head. "Don't worry about it. It's on me."

"You know as a matter of principle that I don't accept anything free from anyone," he said as he left three single dollar bills on the counter. "I'm the mayor. How would it look if I went around accepting things from you on the house?"

"Oh, I don't know; it might look as though you were my friend," I said, but I took the money anyway. "Don't forget your change."

George graciously accepted it, and as he headed out the door, I asked, "Let me know if you find Tommy, okay?"

"Sure thing. Just don't spread what I told you about him around town."

"You know that I'm going to tell Jake, but that's it," I said.

"I figured as much. Okay. Talk to you soon, Suzanne."

After George was gone, I marveled at the story he'd just told me. Why hadn't I heard about Tom's arrest and incarceration when it had happened way back when? Sure, our lives had gone in different directions, but it still surprised me to learn of the life he'd led after we'd parted ways. Just when I thought there was nothing else I could ever learn about the townsfolk of April Springs, something happened to prove just how wrong I was.

George was barely out of sight when I reached for my cell phone and called my husband. He needed to know about this latest development. I probably should have called Chief Grant first, since he was officially handling the case, but I'd let Jake do that. No doubt our police chief already knew about Tom's record, but he might not know about the possible connection between him and the missing newsman.

"Hey, do you have a second?" I asked when he answered my call.

"Sure. Sorry I haven't called you, but I'm striking out everywhere I look."

"I just found something out that might be helpful," I said. "George Morris came by the donut shop, and he told me something in confidence that you should know."

"Hang on a second. I don't want you to violate his trust on

my account, Suzanne," Jake said, stopping me before I could say anything else.

"I've got his permission to share it with you, but only you."

"Am I bound to that as well?"

After I thought about it for a few seconds, I said, "I don't see why you would be. It's not exactly a secret. Just before Ray disappeared, he called George and asked him about Tom Thorndike."

"Your grade-school crush?" he asked me lightly. I'd forgotten I'd told him about Tom long ago.

"Hey, we went out in high school, too," I said.

He must have heard the edge in my voice. "Sorry, I didn't mean to make fun of you. What about him?"

"It turns out that Tom went to prison for robbing a gas station just before we all graduated from high school, and George was the one who arrested him."

"You never told me *that* part of the story," Jake said, his tone going from playful to serious in an instant.

"That's because I didn't know about it. Somehow it escaped the town's gossip mill, if you can believe that. Anyway, Tom came back into town a few months ago flashing a lot of money around. He bought a new truck with cash, and that made Ray suspicious."

"Does George think the two of them may be connected?"

"He seems pretty sure that they aren't, but I'm not convinced myself. Apparently Ray found out that George had befriended Tom while he was in jail, and he called him around six yesterday, digging into Tom's background. Anyway, I thought you should know."

"Thanks for calling, Suzanne. It's a solid lead."

"Just be careful, okay? Remember, you're not a cop anymore."

"You don't need to remind me of that. I'm painfully aware of the fact each and every day," he said. Was there a wistful tone in his voice as he said it? I had a feeling that my husband missed being in law enforcement, but he'd never come right out and said anything about it to me. I didn't ask him, either. I figured if he wanted to talk about it, he knew where he could find me.

In the meantime, I had donuts to sell. My customers were starting to make their way into Donut Hearts, and I aimed to do my best to take care of them.

CHAPTER 3

HALF AN HOUR LATER, JAKE came into the shop. The expression on his face told me everything that I needed to know. Something had clearly happened, and it was bad.

CHAPTER 4

"RAY'S DEAD, ISN'T HE?" I asked Jake as I slumped back against the display case.

"No."

"Tom, then?"

Jake nodded. "They just found his body at the bottom of Laurel Falls."

Laurel Falls was a small cascade that could barely be called a waterfall, though I knew that there was a twelve-foot drop from the edge that led straight down to the rocks below. It managed to make quite a racket as it hit the bottom, but I'd never thought of it as being particularly deadly, though there were posted signs to that effect all along the trail up to it, and the small collection pool above where the water collected before it fell. "That's terrible. Did he fall over the edge from above?"

"That's what it looks like, or so the police chief told me on the phone a minute ago. If it's any consolation, it appears that he didn't suffer. He must have slipped on the wet rocks above the falls and gone over the edge. If I had to guess, based on what I heard from the police chief, his neck must have broken instantly. Those rocks can be tricky, especially in the evening."

"How can they be so sure that it happened last night? He could have been there for a while." The thought of his body bobbing up and down in the falling water made me shiver. Sometimes it felt as though Death had zeroed in on April Springs, and I could feel a target itching on my back every now and then myself.

"It turns out that Gary Timberlake was there last night just before dark, and he didn't see anything."

"What was Gary doing out there by himself?" I asked. Gary was a senior at the high school, and though he had a fondness for my donuts that neared obsession, his young metabolism seemed to burn the calories up as fast as he could consume them.

"Who says he was by himself?" Jake asked me with a shrug.

"Who was with him?" I asked. Gary was a bit of a ladies' man, so it didn't surprise me that he'd visited the bottom of the falls with a girl. I was curious about his latest conquest, not out of some prurient interest, but because whoever was there could back up his story.

"He's not saying. I give him chops for keeping her name out of it. Maybe honor isn't completely dead."

"Maybe," I said. "That still doesn't explain what Tom was doing at the top of the falls all by himself with darkness approaching."

"I'm not convinced that he was by himself any more than Gary was," Jake said.

"What makes you say that? Jake, do you think someone might have pushed him?"

"I don't know, Suzanne," he said as he rubbed his chin in thought. "Maybe it's nothing more than my gut wanting this to be something more than it is, but it seems unlikely that Tom Thorndike would be there alone, especially that time of evening."

"Do you think he was meeting a woman as well? It might make a lovely rendezvous, if you found a woman who wasn't afraid of a hike."

"There's no reason to suspect that he wasn't there on a romantic mission as well," Jake said simply.

"But you don't think so, do you?"

"Woman, get out of my head," my husband said with the hint of a grin.

"Jake, you don't think it's possible that *Ray* pushed him off the edge, do you?"

"Suzanne, I'm not even going to speculate about that. All I know is that Ray Blake is still missing, and now Stephen Grant has a dead body on his hands."

I handed him some coffee and a plain cake donut. "Here you go. You look like you could use something."

"I won't say no to any of your treats," he said as he took a big bite and then washed it down with a gulp of coffee. "Anyway, I wanted you to know what happened before you found out from someone else. I'm sorry. I know that once upon a time, he meant something to you."

"I appreciate that. It's not as though I knew him anymore, but it still makes me sad."

"I get that," Jake said as he finished his donut and polished off the coffee as well. "I'd better get back to the search for Ray, now more than ever."

"Why the rush?"

"The newspaperman is still missing, and now the police are going to be tied up with investigating what happened to Tom. That cuts the search party dramatically, and I know that Sharon and Emma are going crazy with worry."

"You're a good man. You know that, don't you?"

"If you say so," he said sheepishly. "Thanks for breakfast."

"You're very welcome. Let me know if you find anything about Ray," I said.

"You bet."

After Jake was gone, there was a bit of a lull, and I had time to ponder what might have really happened to Tom. Had it been an accident, or was Jake right? Could someone have pushed him? It seemed odd to me that Tom would decide to go hiking to the top of a waterfall as darkness approached, especially alone. Had someone gone with him, or had he been meeting someone there? For a surreptitious meeting, it wasn't as bad a place as it might have seemed at first. After all, though there was a narrow path that led to the top, the common spot to observe the waterfalls was at the base, where the water made its dramatic tumble back into the stream. It would be difficult to see anyone above unless they were standing on the very edge, and the sound of the falling water alone would have made overhearing a conversation up there difficult. But who would want to see Tom dead? Was it about the money he'd come into, as these things sometimes were, or perhaps it was from an unsettled account in his past? I hated to think that it might be true, but could Ray have been the one meeting him up there? Had they struggled, and had Tom fallen back, or could it have been something more deliberate, more sinister? I didn't want to think of the possibility that Emma's dad might be mixed up in what had happened to Tom, but I couldn't exactly rule it out, either.

I was pulled from my thoughts by the front door opening as some of the members of the search party started straggling into the shop. They were all full of talk about the discovery of Tom's dead body, but there wasn't much mention of Ray's absence at all. No one had put it together yet that they might be connected, and I hoped that Ray would be found alive before anyone did. I'd been the cause of suspicion coming from the town in the past myself, and I knew how hard it could be, not only on me but on my family as well.

That just left me with one burning question.

If Ray was innocent, then where was he?

CHAPTER 5

"DID YOU HEAR THE NEWS?" Marla Humphries asked me after walking into the donut shop an hour later.

"Are you talking about them finding Tom Thorndike's body at Laurel Falls?" I asked her.

Marla waved a hand in the air. "That's old news, Suzanne. Ray Blake is in the hospital. He's been found."

"The hospital? What happened to him?"

I wasn't even positive that Marla had come into the donut shop to order anything, though she'd been known to place large orders in the past. She loved being the first to deliver gossip, and it wouldn't have surprised me if she were going door to door. "Nobody knows for sure."

"Marla, why is he in the hospital?"

"Apparently he got conked on the head with a rock, and he can't remember a thing about the last twelve hours! Can you imagine?"

"I can't," I said, wondering if my husband had heard the news yet. "Can I get you anything, Marla?" I asked her before I called Jake.

She looked at the display cases and then shrugged. "Sure. Give me half a dozen donuts, your choice."

"It's not much more to go ahead and get a full dozen," I

Jessica Beck

prompted her. I wanted to find out about Ray, but I still needed to make a living.

"Okay. A dozen it is. Make it quick, though. I've got other errands to run," she said as she pulled her wallet out and slid a twenty across the counter.

I boxed her donuts, made her change, and the second she was out the door, I got out my cell phone to call Jake.

It rang in my hand before I could make the call, though.

"Suzanne, they found Ray," my husband told me.

"I just heard. How bad is he that he has to be in the hospital?"

There was a puff of air on the other end of the line. "How could you possibly have heard about it that quickly? I just found out myself three minutes ago."

"You know how fast news spreads in this town. I understand he has no memory of the last twelve hours."

"It's more like fifteen or sixteen," Jake said. "The chief told me that the last thing Ray remembers is his phone conversation with the mayor around six yesterday, so at least that jibes with what the man told you. I'd love to know what Ray was up to between then and when they found him wandering around the highway a little bit ago. A passing truck driver nearly ran him down. Anyway, I'm on my way to the hospital right now."

"Are you working on the case in an official capacity?" I asked my husband. While he'd turned over the police department to the younger chief, I knew that Stephen Grant still consulted with Jake occasionally, and my husband never did anything to discourage that behavior.

"No, not officially."

"But you're digging into it nonetheless? Shouldn't you leave it up to the police?" I knew it was ironic even as I spoke the words, since I was a world-class meddler in police business myself.

"Hello, pot," Jake said with a laugh.

"You don't have to point out my inconsistencies to me," I

22

said with a laugh. "I just don't want you to hurt your friendship with Stephen Grant. After all, if you two are on the outs, it's going to cause tension between Grace and me, and I'd like to avoid that if at all possible." Grace was not only my best friend, but she'd been dating the new police chief for some time, and the four of us often did things together in our spare time. They were our "go to" couple, and when they weren't available and we were in the mood to socialize, the next couple we tapped were my mother and her husband, the former police chief of April Springs. It seemed that a great many people I associated with were, or were involved with, folks with a history in law enforcement, a set of coincidences that wasn't lost on me. My ex-husband, Max, had offered to do something with us socially along with his steady girlfriend, Emily Hargraves, but while I'd gone a long way toward forgiving Max for cheating on me and being a lousy husband in general, that didn't mean that I was ready to go out to dinner with him and his new girlfriend. I prided myself on being an evolved human being, but I felt as though that was asking way too much of me.

"No worries," Jake said. "It's the oddest thing, but Ray's been asking for me by name since they found him. Evidently he's insisting on my presence at his bedside, even though we've butted heads more than once in the past. I was going to refuse to go, but Emma herself called me and begged me to do it, and we both know that I can't seem to say no to that girl."

"She can be pretty persuasive," I admitted. "Would you like me to close the shop early and go with you?"

"Thanks, but I can handle the newspaperman by myself. Besides, you two aren't exactly best friends either, are you?"

"No, but I'd still do it for you." And Emma and Sharon as well, but I didn't see any reason to add that, since Jake alone was reason enough.

"I'll manage. How's business?"

I was about to tell him that I was experiencing a lull at the moment when I saw half a dozen folks nearing the door. From the look of them, they'd been out all morning searching for Ray, and now that he'd been found, they were in need of my special treats. "It's picking up even as we speak," I said. "Let me know how it goes."

"I will," he said, and then he hung up.

The search party seemed to be in a pretty jovial mood, and I wondered if they'd heard about Tom's body being discovered yet. If they hadn't, I wasn't about to be the one to tell them.

Let them enjoy their high spirits a little longer while they still could.

In the end, it turned out to be one of my busiest days ever, and I ran out of donuts by ten. Since there wasn't time to make more, I was resigned to shutting down early when Grace showed up. She frowned at the barren display cases the moment she walked inside. "You're out of donuts already?"

"What can I say? I had a good run. Sorry about that."

"No worries on my part. How long would it take you to whip up more?" she asked.

"The yeast donuts take too long, but I could make more cake donuts and have them ready in twelve minutes," I said. They wouldn't be fancy, but they'd be fresh, hot, and iced in that time.

"Go do it," Grace said.

"I can't. I've still got customers coming in for coffee and hot chocolate, and I need to top off their coffee cups. I can't just disappear on them like that."

"You won't," she said as she grabbed Emma's apron. "I'll handle the front myself. Now scoot."

Grace had her own job, working as a supervisor for a big cosmetics company, but her hours were flexible, to say the least, and it was a truly kind gesture for her to offer to pitch in like that.

I might have tackled it if Emma were there, but it wasn't fair to make Grace do it. "I can't do that to you."

"Hey, I volunteered, remember?" She turned to my patrons, where all of the tables and chairs were full of customers nursing their beverages of choice. "If Suzanne made more cake donuts and iced them, would you all buy them?"

There was a cheer from the crowd, and as it died, Mitchell Bloom said, "I will if you make mine orange cake."

"There's no time for special orders, Mitchell," Grace said, and then she turned to me. "Right?"

"Not unless you buy six dozen," I said with a grin. I'd gone to a school dance with Mitchell when I'd been sixteen, but that had been our one and only date. He was nice enough; we just hadn't clicked. It worked that way sometimes.

Mitchell smiled, walked up, and slapped a fifty-dollar bill on the counter. "It's settled, then. I'll take six dozen."

There was a groan from the crowd, and another customer said, "I'm not all that fond of orange, to be honest with you."

"How about if it were free?" Mitchell asked him with a grin. "I'm buying until they run out."

"What happened, Mitchell, did you win the lottery?" someone asked him.

"No, but if I can't buy donuts for my friends, what good am I?" He turned to me and grinned. "What do you say, Suzanne?"

"I'm on it," I said. I mouthed a quick "thank you" to Grace, and then I got busy. After mixing the batter for the first six dozen orange cake donuts, I started dropping rings into the hot oil. It was still warm from earlier, so fortunately I didn't have to wait long for it to come back up to temperature, as opposed to if I'd tried to do it first thing that morning. I delivered the trays as they were iced and ready to go, and as soon as those were finished, I made six dozen more of the plain cake donuts. They wouldn't be on someone else's tab, but it would be nice to offer my customers an alternative.

After the orange treats were gone and the regular cake donuts were ready, both iced and plain, I relieved Grace with a smile. "Thanks. You, my friend, are a rock star."

"Happy to help. Should we settle up now about my pay?"

I hadn't expected her to ask to be paid, but it was a perfectly reasonable request. "Sure thing," I said as I hit the NO SALE button on the register and pulled out a twenty. "Would that work for you?"

She laughed. "I don't want your money, Suzanne. I was thinking of taking a dozen of those donuts to go. Stephen's got to be starving. Oh, and I'll take four coffees too, if you think I earned them as well."

"That and more," I said as I got her order together. "Do you need any help with these?" I asked her.

"No, I'm sure Mitchell will be glad to lend me a hand," she said as she smiled at the recent donut benefactor. "Right, Mitchell?" she asked him.

"Anything for you and Suzanne," he said. "You two always were my favorites."

"I don't suppose it hurts you to dream," she replied with a friendly smile.

"I'm glad, because it's all that keeps me going some days," Mitchell said as he pitched in to help.

As she started to walk out the door, Grace said, "Suzanne, I've got scads of paperwork to do, but maybe we could get together later around four. Do you have any plans?"

"Not that I know of, but you know me. There's always a chance that I'll be up to something by then, especially if I'm going to be left unsupervised."

"You wouldn't be my best friend if that weren't true. I'll give you a call later."

"Bye. And thanks again."

"It was my pleasure."

Not long before closing, the mayor came back to the donut shop. Two visits in one day was some kind of record for him, but I knew the moment I saw his face not to tease him about it. "You heard the news about Tom, didn't you?" I asked him.

"Yes. That's why I'm here."

"I'm sorry you lost your friend, George. An accident is a terrible way to lose someone you care about."

"I'm not so sure that it was an accident," the mayor said after he looked around the nearly empty shop.

"Is that your cop's instincts talking? Jake said the same thing to me earlier."

"I just wish I could get Stephen Grant on board," he said. "He thinks Tom slipped and fell over the edge of the falls, but it doesn't make sense to me."

"You're his boss. Can't you make him take your theory seriously?"

"That's the thing," George said. "I can't tell him what to do any more than I could lead Jake around by the nose when he was running things. It's time for some unusual measures."

"What did you have in mind?" I asked, suspecting that I knew exactly what he was about to propose.

He didn't disappoint me when he suggested, "I want you and Grace and Jake to look into what happened to Tom, unofficially, of course. You know this town better than anyone else, and what's more, people talk freely to you, Suzanne. They'll tell you things that they'd never tell anyone during the course of an official police investigation. There's just one catch, though."

"What's that?"

"I have to be involved," he said firmly.

"I thought we'd covered that in the past. The mayor shouldn't get involved in this kind of inquiry, and you know it."

George's face grew red for a moment before he said loudly, "This was my friend, Suzanne. Frankly, I don't care how it's going to look to the voters. I'm helping."

"Okay, but won't it make Stephen look weak to the rest of April Springs if you do something that contradicts his working theory of what happened?" I knew that George genuinely liked our new police chief, and he wouldn't do anything intentionally to undermine him.

"I'm not saying that I'm taking the lead," George explained reluctantly after catching his breath for a moment. "All I'm saying is that I want to play my part. Do you think Jake and Grace will go for it?"

"I can't imagine either one of them turning us down," I said. "You do realize that you might not be happy with what we find, don't you?"

"What do you mean?"

Did he really not see where I was going with this? "Come on, George. You were a cop for a lot longer than you've been the mayor. When we start turning over stones, there's no telling what we might find."

"If that happens, then so be it. I just don't want the questions to go unasked."

I didn't even have to think about it. My friend was hurting, he was asking me for help, and I knew that I might be able to give him a little peace of mind, no matter what we found. "Okay, we'll do it."

"Is it really as simple as that?" he asked me. "I thought I might have to twist your arm, given the fact that you are friends with the chief, and Grace is dating him. It might make things awkward between you all."

"If it does, we'll worry about that when and if it happens," I said. "If you really mean to help, I've got an idea where you can start."

"Anything. All you have to do is ask."

"Where was Tom living? And more importantly, can you get me inside?"

"That I can manage," he said with a grim face. "I was putting him up in a little cottage I own outside of town until he could get things settled and find a place of his own." The mayor frowned for a moment, and then he added, "I know how it might look to some folks that I was harboring an ex-con, but like I said, I don't care. He did his time, Suzanne. That means a clean slate as far as I'm concerned."

"Do you think there'll be any problem with me checking it out as soon as I close?"

"No, Stephen's already done a quick sweep of the place, and he brought my key back to me. Since he's convinced that it was an accident, he didn't seem too worried about it."

"Let me have the key," I said, reaching out my hand.

"Not so fast. I'm going with you," George said firmly.

"Isn't it going to get a little crowded in there with the two of us, Grace, and Jake as well?"

George considered that for a moment. "Tell you what. Let's go check it out together first by ourselves. After we finish up, we can let them know what we find."

"I don't know," I said. "I feel strange leaving them out."

"Tell Jake if you'd like, but if Grace finds out what we're up to before we look around, chances are good that she's going to tell Stephen. He might not feel so charitable toward either one of us, even if he doesn't believe Tom was murdered."

"The truth of the matter is that I don't like keeping secrets from her, either," I said firmly. "We need to face facts. The police chief is going to find out sooner or later."

"That's fine by me. Let's just make it later rather than sooner."

I didn't want to get into an argument with George about it. "Okay. Just this once, we'll do it your way."

"Why do I have the impression that this is going to be your lone concession?"

"I'd say it's because you're a pretty perceptive fellow," I said. "If I'm going to be looking into what happened to Tom, then I'm going to have to do it my way. I know you were a cop, and so was Jake, but as you said yourself, I have a knack for this type of investigation, and so does Grace. You two bring your own skills to the table, but this might not be so cut and dried. I need to make my own impressions and follow the leads that I think might be important. If you and Jake want to lead a retired-cop investigation by yourselves, there's no reason we can't work parallel on this."

"This isn't some kind of game where we're dividing up teams," George said, adding a little heat to his voice. "A man was murdered, Suzanne."

"Or he had an accident," I reminded him gently. "That's what we're going to try to find out, isn't it?" I asked him pointedly. With the mayor, I'd learned over time that I had to stand my ground, or I was in danger of being trampled.

George pursed his lips a moment before speaking, but when he did, much of the tension had already left his face. "What I want to know is when did you get so tough and bossy?"

"I think it was always there," I said, matching his smile with one of my own. "What can I say? Experience has been a great teacher. There are times when I wish I'd never gotten involved in that first murder investigation, but it's too late for regrets now. I've gotten pretty good at it, but if I've learned anything, it's that

I have to follow my instincts, no matter how illogical they might seem to others. Can you live with that?"

"We'll see, won't we?" he asked lightly. "Should I pick you up at eleven and we can get started?"

"Sorry, but that's just when I close. I've got stacks of dirty dishes in back. You'd better make it noon, and you might have to hang around even at that. There's just one thing that I ask."

"What's that?"

"Don't go over there first without me," I said solemnly.

"Not even for a quick peek?" George asked me.

So, I'd guessed right. "No, not even that. I mean it, Mr. Mayor."

"Okay. I won't go until you're with me. See you then. And Suzanne?"

"Yes?"

"Thanks. You're a good friend."

The sentiment, rarely expressed, was sweet to hear. "You, too. See you at noon."

After he was gone, I considered calling Jake and Grace, but I knew that I'd been right before. If the cottage was as small as George had said, we'd be stumbling all over each other, even with just the two of us. Besides, Jake was at the hospital talking to Ray, while Grace was home doing stacks of paperwork.

It wouldn't hurt leaving them out of the investigation for now.

At least that's what I kept telling myself, hoping that somehow I'd find a way to manage to believe it.

CHAPTER 6

B Y THE TIME I CLOSED the shop for the day at eleven, I had just one donut left from the second batch I'd made of cake donuts. It was still so fresh that there was no way that I was going to just pitch it out. I glanced around, couldn't see anyone watching me from the outside, so I took a bite for myself. Wow, it was really good. Sometimes I forgot just how tasty a plain old-fashioned cake donut could be. No wonder so many of my customers liked them. Pouring myself a little hot chocolate to go with my own special treat, I plated the remaining donut and took it and my beverage to a table, giving it a quick wipe down first, and then I sat down to enjoy myself for a minute or two before it was time to tackle that mound of dishes. I was going to be at the shop for a while, so why not take a break before I had to tackle the mound of dirty dishes in the kitchen? I'd have to rush so I could be ready when George came by in an hour to collect me, but I was going to steal a moment for myself first.

There was a rapid knock at the door, and before I even looked up, I said loudly, "Sorry, we're closed."

"I certainly hope so," Momma said from the outside. "Let me in, Suzanne. It's getting chilly out here, and I didn't wear a proper winter coat."

It was only October, just the beginning of our chilly weather in April Springs, but it seemed as though the older my mother got, the less she liked cold weather. I'd worried recently that she might leave April Springs for good for warmer climes, but she'd assured me that she and her relatively new husband were there to stay. As Momma had put it, she was going to play out her hand and stay in the place where she'd been born, raised a family, buried a husband, and reset her life with Phillip Martin. It gave me great comfort knowing that she'd be around if I needed her, even if she did have the capacity to be overprotective of me at times.

"What brings you by the donut shop?" I asked her, trying to hide the now-empty plate where the last donut had so recently resided. "I can offer you coffee or hot chocolate, but I'm afraid that we're all out of treats."

"It's just as well," she said as she looked around the dining area. "Suzanne, this place looks dreadful."

I looked around at the dirty tables and nodded in agreement. "Emma was out looking for her father all morning, so I've been running the shop by myself today. Things kind of got away from me."

My mother's dour expression lightened immediately. "I'm sorry. I should have realized that." After taking off her light jacket, she grabbed the nearest plastic tub we used to transport dirty dishes to the back.

As she reached over me and retrieved my empty plate, I asked, "What are you doing?"

"What does it look like? I'm pitching in," she said cheerfully. "I'll take care of the tables; you go get started on the dishes. I presume there are dishes in back that need to be washed as well. Am I right about that?"

"Yes, but you don't have to help."

My mother put the tub down and patted my cheek. "I know that, but it would please me to do it. Now let's get busy. Don't you worry. Between the two of us, we'll knock this out in no time."

I never would have called my mother for help, and I hadn't been that thrilled at first when she'd decided to pitch in, but as I began washing dishes in the kitchen sink, I realized that I was glad that she was there with me. Since she'd moved out of the cottage we'd shared after getting married, Momma was less a part of my daily life than I liked. There didn't seem to be a happy balance in our situation. We were either tripping all over each other, or we didn't see one another at all for days.

As I added another clean dish to the drying rack, Momma put another tub down and grabbed a towel. "Why don't I get started drying these so you'll have more space?"

"Sounds good to me," I said.

"Suzanne, if you'll tell me where to put things, I'll try not to rearrange anything if I can help it," she answered with a grin.

"It's a deal. So, what brings you by Donut Hearts? Not that I'm not happy to see you."

"I wanted to tell you that Phillip and I are going to Sarasota."

"Florida? For good? You're moving?" I asked her incredulously. She'd already talked about leaving town once. Had she revisited the prospect again and decided to go through with it this time?

"No, not for good; just for a few weeks. My friend, Ruby Hall, made it into a galleried art show down there, so Phillip and I are going down to celebrate with her. It will be nice seeing her again, but we'll be back before you know it. April Springs is home, Suzanne."

"I'm glad to hear it," I said. "If you need to go get ready, I can handle the rest from here."

"Nonsense. We aren't leaving until morning. I wanted to fly, but Phillip likes driving, so we're going by car. It's going to take us quite a bit longer, but as he pointed out, we have the time, so why not?"

My mother had definitely mellowed out since marrying the retired chief of police. In years past, she would have never given in that easily. "Have you heard about Tom Thorndike?" I asked her.

Her lips pressed into two simple lines. "Yes. It's tragic, isn't it? He was always sweet on you, you know."

"Mother," I said. "That was a long time ago."

"Perhaps, but a boy never forgets his first love," Momma said. She added with a slight smile, "I remember when he used to hang around the park just hoping to catch a glimpse of you."

"Until Cindy Bottoms hit puberty, anyway," I mumbled softly to myself, forgetting for a moment that when it came to me, my mother could hear things that most normal humans would miss completely.

"Poor, sweet Cindy. It must be difficult when middle school is your finest hour. Don't pout about it, Suzanne. It was a very long time ago."

"So it was," I said. I knew she was right, but sometimes it was hard to let past transgressions go, no matter how long ago they should have faded into memory. "What a horrid way to die."

"Falling off a waterfall must have been terrifying. Can you imagine what must have been going through his mind as he plummeted to the rocks below him?"

"It would be even worse if he were pushed," I said without thinking about the ramifications of what I was saying.

Momma stopped drying for a second and stared at me. "Suzanne Hart, are you going to investigate this? I understand the police chief believes that it was an accident."

"Maybe so, but the mayor and Jake aren't so sure. George has asked me to look into it, and I've agreed."

"But what if it was truly an accident?" Momma asked.

"Then it will be a short investigation, and no one would mind that."

"What does Jake say about you getting involved? Surely he's

not keen on you possibly endangering yourself if the mayor is correct in his assumption." Momma glanced at me quickly and somehow read the truth in my expression. "He doesn't know yet, does he? My dear child, you have to tell him."

"I will," I said. "I just haven't had the chance yet. How do you do that?"

"Do what?"

"Read my mind. Stop it, could you? It's really creepy."

Momma smiled at me for a moment before she spoke. "Suzanne, I'm your mother. It's what I do."

"If you say so."

"So, are you going to speak with Jake?"

"I promise to just as soon as he gets back from the hospital," I said as I turned back to my dishes.

She abruptly dropped a small plate onto the floor. It shattered, and the noise it made on impact sounded like an explosion. "Jake's in the hospital? What happened to him?"

As I retrieved the dustpan and broom to clean up the mess, I said, "There's nothing wrong with him. He's visiting Ray Blake."

As I swept up the shards of the broken plate, Momma asked, "Why on earth would he do that?"

"You heard that Ray was missing, didn't you?"

"Yes, but I was told that he was all right."

After I finished cleaning up the broken plate and stored the broom and dustpan back where they belonged, I went back to my dishes. "He's been asking for Jake since they first found him. Evidently he's missing fifteen or sixteen hours of his memory due to a blow to the back of the head."

"That's not good, but what does he expect your husband to do about it? Did he go to medical school at some point in his life, and I wasn't made aware of it?"

"No, he's always been a cop, one form or another, all of his adult working life. I'm not sure why Ray is being so insistent on seeing him. I haven't spoken with Jake since he went to see him," I said as I finished washing yet another mug in the warm, soapy water. I'd considered getting a dishwasher once when I'd been temporarily flush with cash, but ultimately I'd decided against it. There was something tactile about the process of washing dishes, and besides, I couldn't afford one big enough to clean most of my hardware, anyway. It was a good thing I hadn't done it; I'd unexpectedly needed a new roof, and I'd just been able to pay for it with the cash I'd had on hand. It was funny how things worked out that way sometimes.

"But you are going to tell him about George's request as soon as you do, right?"

"Yes, mother," I said obediently.

She dried another dish before she asked, "Suzanne, should I cancel my trip? I'm sure Ruby would understand."

"Why would you do that?" I asked her.

"What if you need me, and I'm in Florida?"

I laughed. "Momma, I'm a grown woman. I'll be fine."

She didn't join my laughter, though. "You may be an adult, but I will still worry about you as long as I'm alive. It's a parent's prerogative. So, do I need to cancel my trip and stay?"

"Thanks for the offer, but between George, Jake, and Grace, I'll be well watched over. Besides, you deserve a vacation. You work much too hard."

"Said the kettle to the pot," she answered, finally smiling. "Are you certain?"

"I am positive. Besides, the police chief is probably right. Tom most likely went for a hike at the top of the falls, it started to get dark, he slipped and fell, and that's going to be the end of that."

She looked at me carefully for a full four seconds before she addressed my comment. "You don't believe it for an instant, do you?"

I wanted to deny it, but there was no way that I could; she was right. "I told you to stop that."

After the dishes were finished, all that was left was sweeping up the front and doing the deposit for the day. I could still manage that, even on my own, and have a few minutes left over before George arrived. "Thanks so much for the help, Momma. You were a real lifesaver."

"Let me just finish up the front and I'll be on my way," she said as she grabbed the broom I'd used on the broken plate earlier.

"I can manage," I insisted.

"I'm sure that you can, but I mean to see this to the end," she answered, even as she began sweeping under the upturned chairs. At least I'd prepped the areas I could beforehand.

I knew better than anyone that there was no use arguing with her, so I let her sweep as I ran the reports on the register and cashed out for the day. Happily, all of the totals matched, and I still had ten minutes to spare.

"Shall I walk you out?" Momma asked me.

I wasn't leaving Donut Hearts, at least not straightaway, and certainly not alone, but I didn't want to tell her that. After all, why give her more reason to worry than I already had? I was saved from answering when there was a new tap on the door. This place was getting busier than when I was open for business.

I hoped it wasn't George, being early as was his custom, and for once, things worked out in my favor. Phillip Martin, my stepfather and the former police chief of April Springs, was standing outside, pointing at his watch. "We need to go, Dot. Bob agreed to look my car over at the shop, but if we don't get over there right now, he won't be able to hold our spot."

"You could always go on without me," Momma said with a laugh.

"Go," I urged her. "You were a tremendous help, but I've got it from here. If I don't talk to you before you leave, have a safe trip. Send me a postcard when you get there."

"Or I could just call," she said with a wry smile.

"I'm sure you could, but when's the last time you sent anyone a postcard?"

"I'm not sure, but I know that it's been donkey years," she said as I unlocked the front door and ushered her out.

Momma wasn't quite ready to go yet, though. After she put her jacket on, she hugged me and whispered in my ear, "Be careful, young lady."

"You, too," I said.

"I'm serious," Momma insisted.

"So am I. Don't fall in love with the area while you're down there, you hear?"

"Loud and clear," my mother replied, and then she kissed my cheek soundly before she and her husband left.

I locked the door as soon as they were gone, only to see George striding up the sidewalk toward Donut Hearts.

It looked as though I'd managed to get everything finished just in the nick of time, and I hoped that my luck would hold for the rest of the day.

Somehow I had a hunch that it wouldn't, though.

CHAPTER 7

"A
M I EARLY?" THE MAYOR asked as I unlocked the
door for him and let him in.

"Not by much. Do you mind if we stop off at
the bank on the way to the cottage?"

"How do you know it's on the way?" George asked me with
a smile. He looked happy to be investigating something again
instead of riding herd on the town of April Springs.

"Since the bank is just down the road, I figure we can make it
on the way to wherever we're going." I grabbed the deposit bag,
flipped off the lights, and then unlocked the door for us. "I'm
ready if you are. You didn't go over there without me, did you?"

"A promise is a promise, Suzanne."

"But you were still tempted, right?" I asked him with a grin.

"Sure I was, but you can't fault me for that, since I managed
to resist the temptation. What do you think we'll find there?"

"I have no idea, but I hope we uncover something that at
least gives us a place to start." After we were outside, I asked,
"Am I riding with you, or should I follow in my Jeep?"

"Why don't you come with me? It will give me a chance to
show off my brand-new vehicle."

"You broke down and bought a new car? This I've got to see."

"Well, it's new to me, anyway," George said with a grin as
he led me to a battered old truck that someone had tried to
camouflage himself. Brown and green splotches of spray paint
covered the truck so completely that I couldn't be sure what the

original paint color had been. Leaves had been held against the body in quite a few sections before the spray cans were used, giving it an artificial woodsy vibe. "Isn't it nice?"

I had to laugh. "Maybe, but I'm not sure that it's appropriate for the mayor of April Springs."

"Are you kidding? This thing will get me more votes than my policy on zoning ever could."

"You're probably right at that," I said. "When did you get to be such a politician?" I asked as I slid in on the bench seat beside him.

"Don't blame me. I like to think that it's your mother's fault."

"She may have set you up to be elected the first time, but since then, it's all been on you."

George started up the engine, and I half expected it to cough a few times before stalling out, but to my surprise, it roared into action instantly. As he patted the dashboard, he said, "It's got good bones, regardless of the paint job."

"I don't have any trouble believing it."

After we stopped off at the bank to drop off my day's receipts, we headed to the outskirts of town in the direction of Maple Hollow. "So, it was on the way after all," I said with satisfaction, since we had to pass the bank to get to our destination.

"I never said that it wasn't," he answered.

"How did you happen to acquire a cottage?" I asked him.

"Believe it or not, I inherited it," George explained.

That was news to me. "Funny, I hadn't heard anything about it."

The mayor grinned before he spoke. "Not everything of note happens at your donut shop, young lady."

"It feels as though nobody's called me young in years, and now it's happened twice in the past half hour," I answered with a smile. "I didn't know you had any family left in these parts."

"She wasn't family; well, not strictly speaking, anyway. We're going to Megan Gravely's old place."

I'd known Megan vaguely, but she'd kept to herself for so long that most folks had been surprised to find out that she'd died the year before and not well before that. "How were you two connected?" I asked him. "If you don't mind me asking."

"I normally don't tell the story, but I'll share it with you," George said after a few moments of silence.

"I don't want you to say something you'll regret later."

"Suzanne, if I can't tell you, then who *can* I tell? You're just about the best friend I've got." It was touching to hear him say that, especially coming from a man who usually didn't share his feelings all that often. "Megan always claimed that I saved her life, and she promised to reward me for it, no matter how much I protested that I had just been doing my job."

"Seriously? What happened?"

George's voice lowered and softened a bit, and there was no playfulness in his manner as he related the story to me. "Back when I was on the force, I was on duty one night when we were shorthanded. I was out patrolling alone, and I saw a black Blazer pulled up in Megan's front yard, the headlights blazing into the house. As I got closer, I heard shouting coming from inside. Megan's ex-husband, Clarence, was a mean drunk from way back, and he'd decided to get a little retribution for Megan kicking him out after his last stint in jail. I walked in on them and saw that he had her by the throat, pinned against a wall. Her heels were off the ground, Suzanne. I gave him a pretty good lick from behind with my nightstick, and he went down fast, dropping Megan in the process. She was pretty distraught, so I called Doc Vincent—he was our town doctor back then—to check her out. Megan was shaken up pretty good, but overall she was okay, at least physically. The bruises on her neck took a while to fade, and she had to wear high collars until they did. The marks he left on the inside were another matter entirely."

How could I have never heard this story before? George was right. Sometimes I thought everything of importance in April Springs happened around me, but there was an entirely different world outside of the donut shop's front door that I wasn't aware of. "What happened to her husband?"

"It turned out that Clarence made quite a few mistakes that night. Not only had he assaulted his wife, but he was also in possession of enough narcotics to put him away for quite a while. As soon as he woke up, which happened pretty quickly due to a bucket of icy water being dumped on his head, I read him his rights and carted him away. The man was just plain nasty to the bone, and I doubt anyone mourned him three months later when another prisoner took care of him once and for all."

"George, you're an honest-to-goodness hero," I said in earnestness.

"That's not the way I see it. I was just doing my job, Suzanne. Any cop would have done the same thing in my place."

"Maybe so, but it still sounds like you got there just in the nick of time."

"I'm sure your husband has stories that make mine look like a church picnic."

I shrugged as I said, "The truth of the matter is that we don't talk much about the bad experiences he had when he was with the state police, but I know you must be right. Sometimes when something triggers his memories, especially late at night, he gets a little quiet. I know not to ask him about it, and before long he manages to deal with it, but I still wish he'd talk to me about it."

"He'll tell you when he's ready," George said. "I wouldn't push him."

"I wouldn't dream of it," I said, surprised that the mayor was offering me advice about my marriage. He wasn't wrong, though. I instinctively knew that Jake was the kind of man who had to come to terms with things in his own way, and if he was quiet and distant, that was just his way of dealing with something. Fortunately that didn't happen too often, but when it did, I respected his mood. It killed me to see anything trouble him, but it wasn't exactly realistic to expect the man to constantly be happy. As it was, he was fairly even tempered, something I appreciated greatly, especially after my time being married to Max, the original drama king.

"Good. Anyway, when Megan died, I found out that she'd left this place to me. I wanted to do the right thing and turn it over to her next of kin, but the only problem was that there wasn't anybody left in her family. It was either take the cottage myself or let the county take possession, and I knew that Megan wouldn't have wanted that, so I accepted it. She left enough in her savings account to cover the tax bills and utilities for ten years, and when Tom came back into town, I naturally thought of putting him up there."

"You're really just a big teddy bear under all that gruff, aren't you?" I asked him with a smile.

"Maybe, but I'd appreciate it if you wouldn't spread it around. I've worked too hard to cultivate my reputation as a grumpy old man to just let it go."

We'd finally arrived. I leaned over and kissed George's cheek before I slid out of the passenger seat. "Don't worry. Your secret is safe with me. Are you ready to go inside? If it's going to be too painful for you, given the fact that your friend just died, I'll be okay searching the cottage by myself."

"No, I'm doing this for him. I want to go in."

"Then let's do it."

The cottage was on the small side, and I wondered if it would comfortably hold more than two people living there full time. If it was more than six hundred square feet, I'd be amazed. I'd been expecting the place to be run down, but to my surprise, the wooden exterior had a fresh coat of white paint, there were flowers planted in front, and the lawn was neatly trimmed. "Did you do all of this?" I asked him.

"No, it was all Tom."

I looked at George to see if he was kidding, but he wasn't. "Are you serious?"

"I wouldn't take rent money from him, but he insisted on paying me anyway, so we bartered a little. If he kept up the yard and touched a few things up, he didn't owe me a dime. The paint was all his idea."

"I thought he had a lot of money," I said, confused by the idea that the man had paid cash for a new truck and yet he couldn't afford rent.

"Maybe so, but I didn't find out about that until later," George said.

"I still can't see Tom doing all this," I said. It didn't jibe with everything I'd been hearing about him, but then I remembered that none of us were just one thing. I honestly believed that there was good and bad in all of us in varying degrees, hearts filled with immeasurable shades of gray, and not clear-cut black or white.

"I asked him about it, and Tom said that his time in jail made him appreciate things more. Fixing this place up made him happy, so I wasn't about to stop him. No matter what he might have done in his life, the man deserved better than he got, Suzanne."

"I agree. After all, that's why we're here, isn't it?" I asked as I patted his arm once. "Let's go inside. Is it this nice inside as well?"

"I'm afraid not. Unfortunately, Tom was better with outside work than the interior. I'd better warn you, it's pretty cluttered in there. Megan was a bit of a hoarder."

"I can handle it if you can," I said as George selected a key on his ring and opened the front door for us.

At first glance, it looked as though someone had broken in and trashed the place, and I wondered who had beaten us there. The place was an unmitigated disaster inside.

The real question was had they taken anything of use to us, or were there still clues hiding in the chaos we were about to dive into?

CHAPTER 8

"It wasn't *always* this bad, was it? Am I right in assuming that someone got here before we could and trashed the place?"

"Well, it wasn't perfect before, but I know that it was a lot better than this," George said as he looked around in disgust before he reached for his phone.

"Who are you calling?"

"Stephen Grant," he said.

"Do you think he or his men did this?" I asked him incredulously. I'd known the police chief for years, and I couldn't imagine the circumstances under which he would have allowed something like this to happen on his watch. George had a point, though. He needed to ask the question, no matter how uncomfortable it might make the police chief feel.

"That's what I'm about to find out," the mayor said, and then he held up a hand in my direction as his call was connected. "It's George. Did your men trash my cottage searching it? Are you sure? What did it look like when you got here? No, never mind. I'll handle it. I'll call you later." After the mayor hung up, he turned to me. "He swears he supervised the search himself, and they left the place the way they found it. It was cluttered but neat, which was how it looked three days ago when I came by to touch base with Tom. Somebody obviously tore it apart looking for something."

"Money is the obvious answer, isn't it?" I asked. "After all,

Tom was flashing cash all around town. Maybe someone saw it, and they took the opportunity to make an easy score once they knew that he wasn't going to be coming back."

"Maybe," George said as he put a table back upright that had been flung to one side.

"What else could it be?" I asked him.

"What if Tom was hiding something more important than money here?" George asked as he looked around. "The person who killed him could have come looking for it after he pushed him over the falls."

"That's a bit of a stretch, isn't it?" I asked him softly.

"At this point we can't know that, and it doesn't do us any good thinking that whatever happened here wasn't related to Tom's death."

"You're right," I said. "How do you want to tackle this?"

He looked around the mess, and then he said, "The truth of the matter is that I've been meaning to clean out the clutter ever since I inherited the place, and now is as good a time as any, if you're game. Why don't we move things out onto the porch as we sort through them? It's going to be a bigger job than you signed up for, so if you want me to, I'll give you a ride back to town, and I'll let you know if I find anything."

"Nonsense," I said, literally rolling up my sleeves. "Let's do this."

"Are you sure?" he asked gently.

"Why wouldn't I be? At the very least, I can help a friend lighten his load in life a little. As far as I'm concerned, that's reason enough to help. Should I call Grace, too? She's doing paperwork at home, but I'm certain that she'd come if we called her."

"I'm not entirely sure there would be room enough for three of us in here," George said as he looked around the tiny combination living room/kitchen/dining area.

"You're probably right. Should we split up, or tackle this room together and save the bedroom for later?"

"Let's work our way from the front door, if you're sure you're okay with it."

"Stop asking me that, George," I told him with a grin. "If you give me too many more chances to quit before we get started, I might end up taking you up on your offer."

He laughed briefly, a sound I was happy to hear. "We wouldn't want that, now, would we?"

"I'm just saying," I replied as I offered a slight chuckle of my own. "Now let's dive in and see what we can find."

Finally, the front living space was clean.

"Are you planning on keeping any of this?" I asked him as I surveyed the mess we'd made of the cottage's front porch. There was a pack rat's collection displayed there, full of old newspapers and magazines, glass soda bottles, half-filled mason jars, fabric scraps, bins of old nails, and more flotsam and jetsam than any one person should ever have. "How could one person accumulate all of this? The place must have been tough to walk through even when it wasn't strewn out all over the floor."

"You'd be surprised. Megan had a system, and it didn't feel all that cluttered when you walked into the place."

"I find that hard to believe," I said. "It must have driven Tom crazy."

"If it did, he never complained about it," George said. "Do you think anyone will want this useless junk?"

"I have no idea. We haven't found anything significant yet, but at least we've put a dent in the front part of the house." The thought of what the bedroom must look like was something I wasn't even allowing myself to consider. If the main living space was any indication, it would take more time to clean it than I had available.

"At least the bedroom isn't like this," George said, as though he could read my mind.

"Are you telling me that Megan was neater in there?"

"No, but Tom got my permission to move all of the junk in there out front. Once we tackle this main living space, it should be downhill from there."

"Sounds good to me," I said, trying to hide my elation at the news. I'd kept my eyes open searching for clues as we'd cleaned, but it had become a bit overwhelming dealing with so much clutter. I considered myself somewhat of a minimalist, but Jake took it to the extreme. This place would have driven him mad. I couldn't even imagine what it would look like if we ever managed to finish.

"Should I call someone to come pick up the first load?" George asked me. "We didn't miss anything out here, did we?"

"My question is how could we possibly know? Who are you going to call?"

"Being mayor has certain privileges," George said with a smile. "I can have the front porch clean in fifteen minutes."

"Wow, that's what I call power," I said with a smile. "Aren't you afraid of using your connections to get something personal done?"

"No, I think folks will let me slide on this one. What do you say?"

"Make the call. Let's get it cleared out," I said.

As George grabbed his cell phone, I took one last look at the things we'd pulled out of the house before it was all taken away.

I was glad that I did, because that was when something caught my eye, something that we'd both missed before.

I leaned down and picked it up. It was a pass to Candy Murphy's gym. That, in and of itself, was no big deal, but when I flipped it over, I saw that it had a sticky note attached to the back.

"*Tom,*

I won't do it, so stop asking me.

Candy."

That was certainly cryptic enough. The only problem was that I didn't know how old the note was, but I was going to make it a priority to ask Candy about it. Grace and I, along with Tom, had gone to high school with Candy long ago. She'd been known for wearing daring and quite revealing outfits then, and the trend had continued into adulthood. I doubted that the woman owned anything other than yoga pants, miniskirts, low-cut tops, and men's work shirts worn as jackets, based on what I saw her wearing around town. The only thing in her defense was that she still had the figure to pull it off, even though it had been quite a few years since her graduation. Candy's gym, once financed by an older and quite married man in town named Leonard Branch, had lost its sponsorship when he'd broken up with her, but she'd somehow managed to keep the business afloat despite the setback. Candy liked to present an image to the world of being cute and ditzy, but I'd long suspected that there was a sharp mind behind all of the makeup and curls. I remembered that Tom had had a crush on her in high school, and I couldn't help wondering what her current connection to him might be.

I couldn't wait to ask her.

Just not yet, though.

CHAPTER 9

I TUCKED THE PASS, ALONG WITH its accompanying note, into my pocket and waited for George to finish his phone call. As he wrapped things up, I did another cursory look around our discards, but nothing else attracted my attention.

George finally finished, and as he put his phone away, he said, "They'll be here within the hour. Did I see you rooting through the discard piles?"

"Yes. I found this," I said as I showed him the gym pass.

"I didn't think it was significant," he admitted.

Without saying a word, I flipped it over and showed him the note on the back.

"Where did that come from?" he asked with a frown as he studied it.

"It was there all along. Don't beat yourself up. It was easy to miss."

"And yet you found it," he said with a heavy sigh. "Suzanne, maybe I've lost my touch for this kind of thing."

"Come on, George. It was one little thing."

"Maybe, but then again, maybe not. What else did I pass over? I saw that badge and didn't even think to flip it over. Suzanne, all I can say is that I'm sorry."

The man was really getting morose, but as I thought about it, I couldn't blame him. I would have probably felt the same way if I'd been the one who'd missed the potential clue. "Let's go back inside and keep working," I said as I touched his shoulder.

"Are you sure you still want me?" he asked glumly.

"There's nobody else I'd rather have working beside me," I told him, and though I wouldn't have minded Jake or Grace there as well, George was a good investigator, and I knew one thing for sure: there was no way that anything else would get past him.

"I'll start on the kitchen if you want the bedroom," George suggested.

"Sounds good to me," I said. "If you find anything, give me a yell."

"This place is so small I could probably whisper and you'd still hear me," he answered with the hint of a smile. It was good to see his dark mood lighten, and I felt better as I started for the tiny bedroom in the back of the house.

The first place I headed was the trashcan. I'd made good finds in them in the past, and I had hopes for this one. Though the bedroom had clearly been searched haphazardly as well, it somehow encouraged me. Whoever had been looking hadn't found what they'd been searching for, or so I suspected. Why else the mess? Since the bedspread didn't appear to have been laundered in quite some time, I decided to dump the can's contents after glancing through it. It was mostly wrappers, wadded-up paper, and the like, so I doubted that I'd make things much worse. As I sorted through the contents, I put the trash back into the can, leaving me a clearer idea of what might be in there. The first thing of interest I found was a quarter section of a torn business card. AKE was all I could see, but soon enough, I had the other three pieces, and I could read it in full.

RAY BLAKE, Managing Editor, *April Springs Sentinel.*

So, Ray had been here, and judging by the state of his business card, Tom had clearly been unhappy about it.

Flipping each piece over in turn, I read a quickly scrawled note on the back in what was most likely Ray's handwriting.

"We Need To Talk."

Was everyone in town leaving Tom notes? This one was clearly different from the one he'd gotten from Candy. He'd left hers intact, but this one had been shredded by hand and thrown away. I was about to call to George when he came into the room with a smile. As he saw what I'd done to the bedspread, it faded quickly into a frown.

"What's going on here, Suzanne?"

"I didn't figure it could hurt anything," I said. "Sorry."

"What, the bedspread? Don't be; it needed a good cleaning before you did that. Did you find something?"

I nodded and pointed to the note. After he read it, he said, "Apparently Tom wasn't very happy about getting that note." George flipped the pieces over and saw that it was one of Ray's business cards. "I didn't think anybody handwrote notes anymore, and now we've found two of them. Doesn't everyone text or tweet or email these days?"

"Apparently not everyone," I said. "What do you think it means?"

"It could be nothing," George said. "We already knew that Ray was after Tom for a story. This doesn't add anything to the investigation."

"Maybe not, but it's still an indicator that all was not well between the two men." I gathered the remnants of the card together for safekeeping and asked him, "What did you come in here for?"

"I found something myself," he said proudly. "Follow me into the kitchen."

I did as I was told, and George led me to an open oatmeal cylinder, the type I got my quick oats in. "I'm guessing that's not on the counter because you got hungry."

"No. I found this inside," he said as he handed me something.

It appeared to be a roll of twenties, rolled into a cylinder of its own and held together tightly with a rubber band.

"How much is it?"

"It appears to be an even thousand dollars," George said.

"Is that all there was?" I asked as I reached for the oats.

"Yes, at least in here. I searched every other container in the kitchen, but I couldn't find any more money. It's not that big a place to look."

He was right. The bedroom, as small as it was, was still larger than the cooking space. It appeared that the only place to eat in the cottage was either standing over the sink or sitting down on the couch and using the coffee table as a serving surface. It wasn't exactly a spot where you could entertain company, though apparently Tom had had his share of visitors while he'd been living there.

"I'm hoping we find more cash in the bedroom," I said.

"I didn't realize we were on a treasure hunt, Suzanne."

"I'm not planning on keeping it. I just figured there would be more, given the way Tom was spending it."

George shrugged. "Maybe whoever broke in found the rest of it and already took it."

"If that were the case, then why wreck the entire cottage? You'd think they'd stop searching once they came across a lot of cash, if that was what they were looking for, and yet the entire place looks as though it has been tossed. It wasn't a very professional job, was it?"

"No. If a real pro had done it, we wouldn't even have known that they'd been here. Unless…"

"Unless what?"

"Unless they wanted us to *think* they weren't pros," he finished. "The question is, how clever is our thief and possible killer?"

"I don't suppose we'll know the answer to that until we

catch them," I said. "Do you want to help me finish searching the bedroom?"

"No, you go ahead. I'll take the bathroom."

I'd popped my head in there a few minutes earlier. It was the tiniest space I could imagine anyone using as a bathroom, and that included some I'd seen in recreational vehicles. "That shouldn't take long."

"You might be surprised," he said.

I went back to the bedroom, but the only other thing I found tucked under one leg of the bed was what looked like the edge of a plain brown wrapper. What it had bound I did not know, but I decided to hold it out, just in case.

George came in just as I was finishing up. "Any more luck in here?"

"No, it's a wash. I'd love to get my hands on his wallet and his cell phone, but I'm guessing the police have them both. How about you?"

"I wouldn't mind seeing them myself."

"I meant your search," I said.

He smiled at me. "I know what you meant." It was a good sign that he was joking with me again. "No, I wasn't able to find any more cash, or anything else of interest, for that matter. Suzanne, it's not going to hurt my feelings if you want to check behind me."

"As a matter of fact, I do, but I expect you to do the same for me. This place isn't all that big. It wouldn't hurt having two sets of eyes checking it out."

"Agreed," he said. "Let's do it."

CHAPTER 10

A FTER ANOTHER HALF HOUR, WE concluded that we'd found all of the clues we were going to at the cottage. George and I finished carrying the remains of junk outside, and once we were finished, the cottage felt quite a bit bigger with only a couch, a chair, a coffee table, a bed, and a nightstand in the entire place. It was amazing how open it felt as we walked through for one last check just as the town garbage collectors showed up with their truck. Tom hadn't had much in the way of personal possessions, so George put them in the back of his truck, though I had no idea what he'd do with them.

"Last chance to stop them before everything is gone," George said.

"No, I'm good. You shouldn't have any trouble renting the place now, especially if you slap a coat of paint on the interior walls and have someone clean the windows."

"The truth is, I don't think I'm cut out to be a landlord," he said. "While we were working, I decided to put it on the market."

"Then it could use the paint and the cleaning, anyway," I countered. "After all, you want to get top dollar, don't you?"

"Sure," he said, clearly distracted by how little we'd found in our search.

I touched his arm. "Don't worry, George. We'll figure this out."

"I hope you're right," he said. "I'll be happy to see the end of this mess."

We went outside and found the truck backing up. After the crew greeted the mayor, they made quick work of collecting what we'd put out for them.

They were just driving away as George's cell phone rang.

"Yes. I'm sorry. I got delayed. I'll be there in ten minutes. Good bye."

"Who was that?" I asked.

"An angry councilman, as if they came in any other flavor. I'm late for a meeting. I'm sorry, but I've got to go. Can I drop you off at your Jeep?"

"Why not? What are two more minutes going to matter?"

After the mayor was on his way and I was back at Donut Hearts, I decided the best thing I could do was go home and take a shower. Not only did I have the invasive scent of donuts all over me, including in my hair, but I'd added quite a few layers of dust and grime while searching and then cleaning out George's cottage. I hadn't heard from Jake yet, but I knew that he'd contact me as soon as he had the chance. I couldn't wait to hear what Ray had so urgently needed to tell him, but I knew that I'd be in a more receptive mood if I were clean. If I was able to add a nap into the mix afterward, I'd be downright cordial.

That wasn't going to happen though, at least not right away.

As I was getting into my Jeep, someone drove up and parked directly behind me, managing to cut me off so I couldn't leave. I turned to look at the driver, prepared to argue if I needed to, but I found a strange man staring at me as he got out of his car. "Sorry about that. Do you happen to know who owns this place?" he asked as he gestured toward Donut Hearts.

"I'm Suzanne Hart, and it belongs to me," I said, joining

him cautiously. He seemed harmless enough on second glance, but I didn't like being hemmed in like that. "You're blocking me in."

"What choice did I have? I didn't want you to get away," he said with a crooked grin. I was certain he'd meant it to be disarming, but there was something about him that I didn't trust.

"I hate to be the one to tell you this, but this is not going to be your lucky day. Move your car now, please." This time I asked him more forcefully. If I had to do it again, I'd have backup on my side, namely, the police.

"Sorry. My mom keeps telling me that I'm not nearly as funny and charming as I think I am. I didn't mean any harm by it. Would you be able to spare me two minutes once I move my car into a proper parking place?"

"I can give you ninety seconds at most," I said without smiling.

He grinned at me as though I had. After moving his car, he rejoined me, and I glanced at my watch. I'd said ninety seconds, and that was what I'd meant. "Your time starts right now."

"How much do you want for the place, Suzanne?" he asked.

"Donut Hearts is not for sale," I said flatly. "Sixty-eight seconds left. Are we finished here, or was there something else you needed?"

"Ma'am, we got off on the wrong foot, and I'm happy to admit that it was entirely my fault. Can we start over? My name is Daryl Lane. I'm looking at businesses and buildings around town that might be for sale."

"Why would you want to buy my shop, or anyone else's, for that matter?"

"Let's just say that I represent a wealthy financier who wishes to remain anonymous at this time. He stopped by your quaint little town last month and decided that he'd like to own some of the property in it. He was especially interested in Donut Hearts. He said that you made the best fritters he'd ever had in his life."

"Thank him for me, but please politely decline the offer."

"You understand that you'd still have a job running the place, right? You'd just report to him. It's actually quite appealing. You wouldn't have any of the responsibilities of paying bills or worrying about profits and losses. You'd just be one of his many employees, punching a time clock every day. He'd handle all of the worrisome decisions."

Wow! That was the worst possible thing he could have suggested to me. I didn't take orders from anyone, not even my husband, and certainly not some stranger! I might not reap a financial windfall with my balance sheet, but I was my own boss, I did as I pleased, and I lived life on my own terms. "If he really likes my fritters, I can make them any day that I'm here, and with enough notice, I can have a dozen ready for him any time he'd like. He can buy all of the donuts he wants, just not the donutmaker."

"I'll let him know," Daryl said. "By the way, I'm sorry for your loss."

"What loss is that?" I asked him, realizing that he was now beyond my original time limit. I decided to be gracious about it, especially since his boss had liked my fritters so much.

"I understand a local man died this morning. John, was it?"

"His name was Tom," I corrected him.

"Yes, that's right. Tom. Did you know him well?"

"I suppose so," I said. "Listen, you've made your offer, I've declined, and now what I'd really like to do is go home, take a shower, and maybe even grab a nap."

"I understand. I'll leave you to it, then."

As I got into my Jeep, I asked him, "Since the donut shop isn't for sale at any price, will you be leaving town now?"

"Oh, no. Not anytime soon," he said with a chuckle. "I'm certain our paths will cross again. It was nice meeting you."

"You, too," I said, though I didn't entirely mean it. There

was something about the man that I didn't like, not that my gut was necessarily always right. Still, I'd tell Jake about him the second I caught up with him again.

I finally managed to drive home unaccosted and jumped in the shower.

As the water started to cascade down on me, I heard the bathroom door slowly open.

Was Jake back home, or was someone else paying me an unexpected and most unwelcome visit?

CHAPTER 11

"I'VE GOT A GUN!" I said loudly before I pulled back the curtain to see who might be out there.

"Well, unless it's waterproof, you're probably going to ruin it," Jake said with a laugh as I peeked out.

"You could have at least announced yourself," I said as I finished rinsing my hair.

"Sorry. Do you need any help with that?"

"No thanks, I'm finished," I answered as I shut the water off and took the towel he offered me. "I wasn't expecting you."

"Funny, I thought I was gone way too long. After all, a little of Ray Blake goes a long way. Are you hungry? Because I'm starving."

I remembered my lone donut a few hours earlier and realized that I hadn't had a proper lunch, either. "I could definitely eat," I said. "What did you have in mind? I know we have eggs, and there's some of that frozen turkey chili I made last week in the freezer." Jake prided himself on his own chili recipe, but it was spicy enough to give my mouth blisters, metaphorically at least. I'd gotten him to compromise, and now we alternated our chili recipes. Over time, I'd gone from ground beef to ground chicken, and lately I'd been happiest with ground turkey.

"No offense, but I was more in the mood for a burger," he said. "After all, the Boxcar Grill is just a few hundred yards away if we cut through the park. What do you say?"

"Sure. Why not? Just give me ten minutes, and I'll be ready to go. You can keep me company in the meantime. What happened with Ray?"

"There's too much to go into right now. If it's okay with you, I have a few phone calls to make before we go." Jake kissed me quickly, and then he headed out to our main living space. He was being awfully cryptic about what he was up to. What had he and Ray talked about? I knew I wouldn't have long to wait to hear the whole story, but it spurred me on to get ready even faster. Six minutes later, hair still wet, I was ready to go. I usually wore it up in a ponytail, but I'd give it a little more time to dry before I pulled it back when we got to the diner.

Jake was still on the phone. He held up one finger toward me, then said, "We'll talk later. Okay. Got it. Thanks."

"Who was that?" I asked him.

"I was just checking on something. Are you ready? Hey, your hair's down."

"Wow, you really are a detective," I said with a smile. "I thought I'd let it air dry before I put it up."

"Aren't you worried about getting a cold? It's still kind of chilly out," he said as he touched my shoulder lightly. I still tingled at his touch, something I was eternally grateful for.

"Okay, now you sound too much like my mother," I said.

"What can I say? We both love you. But never forget one thing: I love you more," he said with a grin.

"What can I say? I just must be loveable."

"Yeah, I'm sure that's it. Are we ready?" he asked as he held my jacket out to me.

"I am if you are."

As we left the cottage we shared nestled on one edge of the park and headed toward the diner, I marveled at how lucky we were to live in such a welcoming place. The leaves were in their full glory, and the park had transformed from a sea of green to a patchwork quilt resplendent in shades of red, gold, and brown.

This was my favorite time of year, with a bite in the air and an explosion of color everywhere I looked. We'd just started having fires again in our fireplace, and the daylight hours were quickly slipping away as the darkness crept in more and more every day.

I zipped my jacket up and realized that Jake had probably been right about my hair. A cool breeze sent a distinct chill through me, and I decided to pull it back even if it was still a little damp. "Now, tell me about your meeting with Ray."

"Funny you should call it that," Jake said.

"Why is that?"

"Suzanne, I'll be happy to tell you all about it, but is there any way we could just enjoy this short stroll through the park, hold hands, and not talk about anything more serious than how lucky we are?" he asked me.

It was a rare burst of overt sentimentality on my husband's part, though he definitely had his moments. "You know what? That sounds really good to me," I said as I felt my hand naturally fit into his. I knew that he was right; we *were* incredibly lucky, but that wasn't the entire story. Marriages take work, no matter how good they are, and we did our share. I'd been jumpy because of my first failed marriage to Max, while Jake had lost his first wife, pregnant with his only child, in a car accident. Somehow we'd found ourselves thrown together, ironically enough by the murder of one of my customers at the donut shop. It was hard to remember the Suzanne I'd been before he'd come into my life; it was as though she were a stranger to me. "Let's have a fire tonight."

He grinned down at me. "I was just thinking the same thing. We really need to set up a fire pit outside. I have the fondest memories of camping in the autumn with my family as a kid and sitting out under the stars as the fire blazed away."

"I'm good with that," I said, though honestly, my idea of a fire was one in the fireplace while I sat on the couch sipping a cup of tea and enjoying a good book. But if it was important to Jake to do it outside, then that made it important to me. "We can get started on it today," I said, though I'd had plans to continue my investigation into what had happened to Tom.

"Maybe we can push it back a little," Jake said reluctantly.

"What are you up to, mister?"

"Let's at least wait until we order," he said. "Besides, we're already here."

We walked up the steps to the grill, a pair of converted boxcars that served as the town diner. Trish Granger, the owner and a dear friend of mine, greeted us at the door. "I can't believe it's already getting cold out, can you?"

"Well, it *is* October," I said, "and besides, we like it."

"I do, too, but it just seemed to come too early this year."

"I don't know. I was under the impression that it *always* came right after September," Jake said with a grin.

"You know something? You're pretty funny for a cop," she told him, smiling back at us.

"Maybe, but I'm not a cop anymore," Jake said.

"So you say." Trish looked around the nearly empty diner. "Take your pick of seats. I'll be there in a second. Would you like a pair of sweet teas, or do you want hot chocolate instead?"

I knew she was making a joke about the cold, but I'd already had a cup of hot cocoa, and generally one per day was my limit. "Tea sounds great," I said.

Jake held up two fingers. "Sounds good to me."

"We can order now, if it's easier," I said, wanting to get Jake alone so he could tell me what Ray had said to him earlier.

"I like it," Trish said with a grin. "It saves me the steps."

"Two burger plates with fries, all the way, please," I said.

"Make that double for me," Jake said with a grin.

"You seriously want two plates apiece?" Trish asked.

"No, you're right. After all, I want to be able to walk out, not be carried out on a handcart. Two plates, one apiece," Jake said.

Trish just chuckled softly as she turned to give the order to the kitchen. "Like I said, you're a funny guy. Hang on one second."

We waited until she placed our orders in back, and then she got us two glasses of sweet tea, without the lemon in either one, which she knew was our preference. "You might as well take these with you, since you're headed that way anyway."

I laughed. "I believe I've created a monster, haven't I?"

"I don't know. Maybe it will catch on, and I won't have to leave the register all day."

"You'd get bored in an hour," I told her. Trish loved mingling among her customers, trading quips and comments with the clientele as she refilled countless glasses of tea and cups of coffee.

"Chances are it wouldn't even take that long," she said.

After we were settled and I'd sipped my tea to make sure it was just as sweet as ever, I looked at Jake. "Okay. You've stalled long enough. Talk to me."

"Suzanne, I've got a job."

CHAPTER 12

"EXCUSE ME? I WASN'T AWARE that you'd applied for one. Are you going back to the state police?" I knew that Jake had grown bored with his lack of a career, but his announcement threw me for a loop. Would it mean that he'd be forced to leave April Springs again? I hated the thought of coming home and finding the cottage empty, but if he needed a job to feel fulfilled, I wasn't about to stand in his way. "You know that I support you completely, but I'm going to hate having you gone."

"Hey, take it easy," he said softly as he reached across the table and rubbed my shoulder gently. "I'm not going anywhere, Suzanne."

"I just assumed you'd be leaving town again for work," I said. "What is there here in April Springs to challenge you?"

"I'm working for Ray Blake," he explained. "I handled this poorly. Should I go back and start over?"

"I wish you would," I said.

"When I saw Ray," Jake said, "he was a real mess. They had to shave part of the back of his head to stitch him up. Somebody smacked him pretty hard with what must have been a rock, and it left a jagged cut. Apparently that's why he's got amnesia. Ray claims the last thing he remembers is his conversation with George Morris last night. The next thing he knew, he was wandering around Viewmont Avenue this morning, dazed and confused."

"Is he saying that he never even saw Tom last night?"

"That's the thing. He claims that he has no idea what happened after he spoke with George."

"Do you believe him?" I asked him.

"I do. If he's lying, he's good enough at it to fool me," Jake said, "and I've had a lot of skilled liars cross my path in my life."

"What exactly does he expect you to do about his situation?" I asked my husband.

"He wants me to recreate his movements from making that phone call to the mayor to being found on the road this morning."

"Isn't that a job for the police?"

"Not even close," Jake said. Was there a twinkle in his eyes as he said it? He was excited about doing this, something I hadn't seen in him for a while. "Stephen has got it in his mind that Tom's death was an accident and that Ray's amnesia is just a coincidence."

"You don't believe that for a second, do you?"

"Suzanne, I was a cop too long to swallow that. The only thing going against Chief Grant is his inexperience. Given time and enough practice, he's going to be a fine chief, but right now, he needs a little seasoning."

"How is he supposed to get it without active time on the job?" I asked Jake.

"That's the point, but the truth is, Ray is afraid that he might have had something to do with Tom's death," Jake told me, lowering his voice.

"Is that possible?" I asked him, softening my tone as well.

"Well, I'm not ready to rule it out," Jake said.

"Isn't he afraid of what you'll find when you start digging?"

"I think he's *more* frightened that he'll never know the truth. I've never been a fan of the man, but I admire the way he's handling this. I know I've made fun of him in the past for his zealous behavior, but he really does want the truth, no matter what it might mean for him."

"So you're acting as a private investigator for him," I said, trying to take it all in. "I never saw you as a private eye."

Jake clouded up at that. "I'm not sure that's what you'd call what I'm doing."

"Funny, it sounds exactly like that to me. You know what? I think it's what you were meant to do. You can still investigate and be home with me at night. Plus, you don't have to take any cases you don't want to investigate." I had a sudden thought. "I've even got an office for you. If you don't mind taking Teresa Logan's place over, you won't even have to pay me rent."

"Let's not get ahead of ourselves," Jake said hastily. "I've agreed to help Ray. Whether I want to do this for a living is another matter entirely."

"Just think about it, okay?" I asked.

"Sure. Anyway, back to Ray. After we eat, I'm going to check out the top of the waterfall and see if I can find any sign that he was there yesterday."

"Do you think Ray might have actually been there when Tom went over the edge?" I asked.

"I honestly don't know, but I figured I'd work my way back from there and see if I can pick up any trace of him in case he was. If that doesn't work, I'll have to start wandering around Viewmont Avenue looking for some clue as to where Ray had come from when he was found."

"I want to go with you to the falls," I said steadily.

Jake looked at me closely before he replied. "Suzanne, why do I get the feeling that this isn't just idle curiosity on your part?"

"It's not. I need to tell you what I've been up to since this morning," I said when I spotted Trish coming toward us, carrying our lunches. "But it's going to have to wait until after we eat."

My husband wasn't pleased about the delay any more than I'd been waiting to hear his news, but food always took precedence. We tried to never let business talk interrupt our meals, so we took fifteen minutes off and enjoyed the food. Trish had recently switched her meat supplier to a local farmer who supplied grain-fed beef, and though her prices had gone up accordingly, I for one was happy to pay the difference. Her burgers, which had been good before, were now works of art in my opinion and Jake's as well.

After we finished eating, Trish brought us two cups of tea to go unbidden, and the check. We didn't typically get dessert, and she knew if we wanted it, neither one of us would have been afraid to ask.

Jake's phone rang, and after he handed Trish a twenty, he said, "Excuse me, ladies. I have to take this."

After he stepped outside, I walked up front and took the change from Trish. "It's terrible about Tommy, isn't it?" she asked. We'd all gone to school together, and it gave me a pang hearing him called Tommy again.

"I know. I still can't believe it."

She lowered her voice. "Suzanne, it wasn't an accident, was it?"

"What makes you say that?" I asked her.

"I'm not sure I should say anything. It's probably nothing. I just wish you were looking into what happened to him. Then I wouldn't mind telling you about it."

"As a matter of fact, George asked me to dig around a little this morning," I admitted. Normally I liked to keep a low profile when I was investigating what could be murder, but I trusted Trish with my life, and I wasn't just saying that.

"Why George?" she asked curiously.

"Evidently they were friends," I said.

"Well, you never know, do you?" Trish asked after whistling

softly to herself. "So then I *can* tell you. I had to come back to the diner three nights ago to get something I forgot when I heard two men arguing in the park. I didn't think much about it at the time, but after what happened to Tommy, it started to haunt me."

"Why? Was he one of the people arguing?" I asked, my senses starting to tingle.

"Yes. I can't be one hundred percent positive, but I'm pretty sure the other one was Mitchell Bloom. They were both in the shadows, so it was hard to be sure, but I'd bet my life that it was him."

"Mitchell? What were they arguing about?"

"It sounded to me like it was about money," Trish said. "Mitchell told him that he was going to get what was owed him, or Tommy would regret it."

"How did Tommy react to that?" I asked, slipping back into calling him by his old name.

"He laughed at him. It infuriated Mitchell, and when Tommy turned his back on him and walked away, I half expected Mitchell to jump him. He didn't, but the whole thing left a bad taste in my mouth, and now I can't stop thinking about it. Suzanne, could he have pushed Tommy over the edge if he didn't get what he thought was coming to him?"

"I don't know, but I'm going to do my best to find out," I said. "Thanks for telling me about it."

"Honestly, I feel better unloading it onto you. If there's anything I can do to help, all you have to do is ask. I keep thinking if I'd only said something or stepped in, none of this would have happened."

I touched her hand lightly. "Trish, you know there's no way that any of this is your fault, don't you?"

"I know that logically, but I still can't shake it emotionally.

I keep thinking that if you figure out what really happened to Tommy, I can get past it, no matter what."

"I'll do my best," I said.

As I joined Jake outside, I was surprised to see that, though he was now finished with his phone call, he was currently being cornered by the nosiest citizen of April Springs, and she was clearly bending his ear about something.

CHAPTER 13

"Hey, Gabby. What's up?" I asked as I joined my husband and Gabby Williams.

"I was just telling your husband what a shame it was about Tom Thorndike," she said. Gabby ran ReNEWed, a gently used clothing shop that offered only the best April Springs had to offer. She was also the self-appointed arbiter of taste and what was right or, in most cases, wrong with our fellow townsfolk.

"I agreed with her, and then I told her that we had an appointment we couldn't miss," Jake said, looking as though he were trapped and couldn't escape.

"That's right. I nearly forgot all about it. We'd better get going," I said, and then I smiled at Gabby. "Besides, shouldn't you be back at your shop?"

"I've decided to close early today," she said. "I like to keep my hours capricious. It keeps my customers on their toes."

It was pretty clear to me that Gabby didn't have any competition if she was able to come and go as she pleased without hurting business. I couldn't afford such a luxury myself. If I didn't open the donut shop one day, the grocery and even the convenience store had things that might be considered by some a substitute for what I sold at Donut Hearts. I didn't think so myself, but it was amazing what some people would settle for if it was cheaper and "sort of like the original." I myself was willing to pay a little more to get a quality product, and I couldn't understand why others would ever accept something inferior just because it was cheaper. "If it works for you, by all means. Come on, Jake. We're going to be late."

"If you had an appointment somewhere, why aren't you driving?" Gabby asked, looking around the parking lot for my Jeep or Jake's truck.

"That's because we have to head back to the cottage first," I said. "Besides, we're trying to help the environment. You know, walking is better than driving and all that."

"Try walking to Raleigh and then get back to me," Gabby said, citing a place four hours away by car.

"No thanks," Jake said as I pulled him along. Once we were out of her hearing, Jake added, "Thanks for saving me."

"Gabby's harmless," I replied.

"If that's true, then why would I rather face an armed killer than deal with her questions?"

"It's because that's what you know," I answered. "I'm assuming our appointment is entirely in your mind."

"That's not true. We have an appointment to check out Laurel Falls, remember?"

I smiled, and then I realized that I'd put it off long enough. It was time to tell Jake what I'd agreed to do while he'd been talking to Ray Blake. "Jake, I'm digging into what happened to Tom Thorndike."

He took it in for a few moments as we walked through the park toward our place before he spoke. "Were you really that close to your ex-boyfriend, Suzanne?"

"I wasn't, but George was." I brought my husband up to speed, up to and including our findings at the cottage where Tom had been staying. "I didn't have any choice, Jake. George needs to know the truth, and I couldn't just say no to him."

"I can see that," my husband said. After a moment, he added,

"I'm willing to bet you didn't exactly fight him on this though, did you?"

"Why do you say that?"

"Suzanne, you have a nose for this kind of thing. I have a hunch that if George hadn't asked you, you would have still found a way to dig into this."

I shrugged. "I won't deny it. If it was an accident, I can live with that, but I take it personally when someone commits murder in April Springs and thinks they can get away with it."

"That's Stephen Grant's job, though, isn't it?"

I stopped in my tracks four steps from our front porch. "Perhaps, but Stephen thinks it was an accident. Who knows? Maybe he's right. But I need more proof than his guess. If I'm wrong, what is it going to hurt?"

"You could alienate some of the town by asking them probing questions," Jake reminded me.

"Please. Some folks get out of bed looking for a fight, so why not give them a reason? Jake, no matter what he may have done with his life, the man still deserves justice. Do you agree?"

"I hate the idea of a murderer getting away with it on general principle just as much as you do," Jake admitted. "I'm just sorry I can't drop what I'm doing and help you."

I softened toward him instantly. "I appreciate the gesture, but you're going to have your hands full with Ray. Besides, I've got George and Grace helping me."

"I'm not sure how much the mayor can do without being accused of using his office for personal gain, but at least you've got Grace. Was she hard to convince?"

"Actually, I haven't talked to her about it yet," I answered with a smile.

"And you're that sure that she'll say yes? Strike that. If you asked her to help you rob a bank, that woman would ask you when and where and if she should bring the masks."

"I'm not quite sure she'd go that far, but she likes being my partner in our investigations."

Jake nodded. "There's no doubt about that in my mind."

"I'm ready to check out Laurel Falls if you are. I just need to call Grace first so she can join us."

"Would you mind holding off on bringing her into this?"

I looked at him oddly. "I suppose I could, but I'm still not completely sure why you're going up there, too. Isn't that the last place you'd be hoping to find a clue about Ray's whereabouts?"

"Of course it is, but hoping and wishing won't make it so. It just makes sense to have a look around and see if there's any indication that he was up there with Tom when he died. Besides, I'll use any excuse to be close to you."

"That's sweet of you to say," I replied, kissing his cheek. "Should you drive, or should I? Do you think your truck can make it?"

"Hey, that's no way to talk about her. She's never let me down."

"Yet," I answered. "How about letting me drive anyway, just for fun?"

"Okay. Fine," he said.

That was when we got into my Jeep, and I started driving toward Laurel Falls.

After parking in the lot near the bottom of the falls, we headed up the hiking trail beside it that ascended to where the waterfall began.

"This is kind of an odd place for a meeting, isn't it?" Jake asked me as we climbed. The path was narrow and overgrown, and at times it came close to skirting the falling water. At other times it meandered through a copse of trees, and all in all, I knew that it would take a little over ten minutes to climb to the top of the falls.

"What makes you think it was a meeting?" I asked him as I dodged a wild thorny vine. There were people who would be able to identify it by sight, know its name in Latin and its common name as well, but I wasn't one of them. All I knew was if a thorn caught my skin, I'd start bleeding, and that was all I needed or cared to know about it.

"Well, if Ray *was* up here with Tom, what else could it have been? Unless he followed him up just so he could push him over the edge."

"Maybe they wanted some privacy," I said as we broke out into the clearing. There was a calm expanse of water before the fall, with pooled water and several rocks and boulders scattered throughout the stream. I couldn't see where the water disappeared over the edge from where we stood, but I could hear the results of the plummeting stream as it hit the rocks below. "They wouldn't have gotten that down at the base of the falls. It's one of the most popular make-out spots in town. Besides, we can't assume that if Tom was pushed, it had to be Ray. There are a handful of other suspects I have in mind besides the newspaperman."

"I get that," Jake said. "At the moment, though, all I care about is whether it was Ray or not. I'll leave the rest of the investigation to you and the police chief."

"My, you've seemed to adapt pretty quickly to your new position," I said with a smile.

"I prefer to think of it as narrowing my focus."

There wasn't crime scene tape or anything to mark the fact that someone had fallen to his death from here the night before. All I saw was one weathered wooden sign citing danger and reminding folks to stay away from the edge. If the police had done much of an investigation where we were, there were no real signs of it.

"Where do you suppose it happened?" I asked as I looked at the nearby rocks with a shiver.

"Judging on where they found the body, I'd say it was right about there," my husband said as he started toward the rocks. Water constantly churned around them, and I saw several splashes even as I watched. It looked precarious to me, but I could see the appeal of it for some. Standing on the rock would give the viewer a nice look at the falls and the pool below.

"Should we really be walking out there?" I asked Jake.

It was too late, of course, since by the time I asked, he was nearly there. "I need to see it for myself. If it makes you nervous, stay here. I'll be right back."

"No, thanks. I'm coming with you," I said despite the growing dread in the pit of my stomach from what I was doing.

We got to the widest and flattest rock he'd pointed to, and we looked down at the water below together. "Why does the drop look so much farther from up here than it did at the bottom?" I asked him, having to raise my voice quite a bit to be heard over the cascading water.

"What?" Jake asked as he turned to me. Raising his voice, he asked, "Did you say something, Suzanne?"

"It looks higher from up here," I said, nearly shouting this time. The noise was loud enough to block out normal conversation, and I wondered if it was from the falling water alone or if there was some other kind of acoustic trick at work. Jake knelt down, studied the rock, and then stood up and turned to me.

"Let's head over there where we can talk a little easier," he shouted as he pointed back to the path where we'd just come.

It was a suggestion I gladly embraced. "I'm right behind you," I yelled.

Even then, I wasn't entirely sure that he heard me. It amazed me that fifteen feet from the edge of the falls, we could almost hold a normal conversation again without screaming at each other. "That explains that," I said.

"What's that?"

"If Tom had been standing on the edge waiting for someone to show up, they could have easily snuck up behind him and pushed him over. He wouldn't have heard them if they'd been singing 'The Star-Spangled Banner.'"

"That's a point," Jake said. There was a bit of mud and plant life beneath our feet, and Jake knelt down to examine it.

"What are you looking for?" I asked him.

"This," he said as he took out a small plastic vial and collected some mud, as well as a bit of the weeds growing there.

"Is it significant?" I asked him.

"I don't know yet, but it could be. I found something on Ray's pants when I checked out his clothes at the hospital, and it looked an awful lot like this," Jake said.

"It could have come from anywhere though, couldn't it? There's a lot of mud in these parts, and plant life is everywhere."

"Maybe, but the leaf I found matches this. I took a photo of it with my cell phone and sent it to a friend who's an expert at this kind of thing. Turns out it was from a plant that grows only near the water." Jake took another picture with his phone and then hit a few buttons. He looked frustrated as he said, "I can't get a signal up here, so I'll have to send it later. Not that it matters all that much. I'm fairly positive it's the same specimen, but I'll get it checked out just to be sure."

"What about the mud?"

"I've got samples of each as well, and another contact who will take a look at them as soon as she gets a little time."

"She?" I asked him, raising one eyebrow.

"Yes, she," he said, not even noticing my jibe. I knew Jake had plenty of friends of both sexes, mostly in law enforcement. If it had been Max, I would have immediately suspected something was going on, but not with Jake. He'd never done anything to indicate that he wasn't worthy of my full and complete trust, and I wasn't about to look at him the same way I had my first husband.

"How soon will you know for sure?" I asked him.

"I don't know. She's on her honeymoon right now, but she'll be back sometime in the next few days. It's going to have to wait until then."

Okay, I felt better knowing that the woman in question had just gotten married. Did that necessarily make me a bad person or even a suspicious wife? I decided not to analyze it either way. "Where does that leave you in the meantime?"

"I keep digging," Jake said, "and so should you. It won't hurt either one of us being able to visualize this later," he said as he snapped several pictures of the water, the rocks, and the land around us with his phone. I followed suit since it was a solid idea, when Jake had a sudden thought. "Suzanne, do me a favor."

"Anything."

"Head back down the path."

"Sure. Let's go," I said.

"I mean by yourself," he replied.

"Why? Did I say something that offended you?" I asked him.

"What? Of course not. I just want to check something out."

A sudden and irrational thought crossed my mind. "You're not going to jump, are you?"

He looked at me oddly for a second before he replied. "Not a chance. I want to see how close I can get to the edge before you can see me at the bottom of the falls."

"Jake, I'm not sure I like this experiment," I said reluctantly. "What if you fall?"

"I'm not going to fall, Suzanne. Would you prefer it if I went down and *you* stood on the edge alone?"

I wasn't all that crazy about either one of us doing it, but if one of us was going to fall, I couldn't bear the thought of standing at the bottom and watching my husband plummet to his death. "Okay. I'll wait up here until you get to the bottom."

Jake shook his head and frowned. "Sorry. The offer wasn't sincere. It was my idea, so I'm going to be the one who does it."

"Fine, just don't step too close to the edge," I said, knowing that it was pointless trying to convince him not to do it. "I'll call you when I can see you."

He held his cell phone up in the air. "I don't have a signal here, remember? We'll have to do it with hand gestures."

"This just keeps getting better and better, doesn't it? I'll see you soon," I said as I took off back down the path. The lack of cell phone service had surprised me. Was it significant to Tom's demise or just something to be filed away in the Useless Information folder? The problem was that I never knew until it failed to matter one way or the other anymore, but I would still keep it in mind. The hike down seemed much longer than it had taken coming up. With just about every step, I had to stop myself from visualizing how many ways this could go wrong. Jake was a grown man, a seasoned cop, and I knew that his question was a fair one. That didn't mean that I had to like it, though.

As I rounded one corner of the steep path, my foot slipped a little, and I felt my legs go out from under me. I found myself being carried off the path away from the waterfall and into the woods. When I put my hand down to stop myself from sliding any farther, I saw something catching the light in the dappled shade.

It was a bit of cloth with a button attached to it that looked as though it might have come off of a man's shirt. Fairly fresh dirt was caked into the buttonholes, and I wondered how recently someone had lost it on this path. I pulled out my bandana and carefully placed it inside before I folded it back up and stuck it in my pocket. I'd have to share it with Jake once he was back down at the bottom with me.

If he didn't go over the edge himself.

CHAPTER 14

"**I** CAN SEE YOU NOW," I shouted at Jake ten minutes later from the pool of water below. I was waving my hands over my head, and he glanced down and smiled before backing away from the lip of the falls.

Nine minutes later, he rejoined me at the base of the falls. "Wow, that was a little hairy, if I say so myself."

"What did you have to do?" I asked him.

"Relax. I was okay," he said as he stared up at the falls, "but I had to go to the very edge before I could see you below. If anyone saw Tom up there, it had to be just before he fell."

"Is that significant?" I asked.

"I don't know yet. It could be, but we'll have to wait and see. One thing is certain; if someone did push Tom over the edge, nobody would have been able to see it from where you were standing. Are you ready to go?"

"Not just yet. I found something myself on the way down the path," I said as I pulled out my discovery.

He noticed my dirty jeans. "What happened?"

"I slipped on the path. It's not important. This is," I said as I held it out toward him.

Jake didn't touch it, but he took the entire bandana from me and studied the button and cloth. "Where did you find this?"

"Like I said, I slipped on the way down and ended up right beside it," I admitted, not happy about revealing my clumsiness. "Is it Ray's?"

"No, I checked his clothing out carefully. All of it was intact," he said as he handed it back to me.

"It's fairly recent though, wouldn't you say?"

"I'd guess so. The tears of the material are still fresh, and the mud caked onto the button hasn't entirely hardened yet. It was in the shade, wasn't it?"

I nodded. "How did you know that?"

"If it had been in the sun, the mud on it would have hardened in an hour," Jake answered.

That thought hadn't occurred to me. "Sometimes I forget just how good you are at this," I said.

"Used to be, at any rate," he said.

"Still are," I answered. "What should I do with it?"

He pulled a plastic evidence bag out of his pants pocket. "Let's put it in this until we know if it's significant or not."

I wasn't at all surprised that he'd brought evidence bags with him. I slid the cloth and button from my bandana into the bag, and Jake sealed it before handing it back to me. "There you go."

"You don't want to keep it yourself?" I asked him.

"No need to. It's not part of my case."

"Should I turn it over to the police?" I asked him.

"If it were me, I would, but it's your find, so it's up to you." The implication was clear in his voice, though.

"I'll give it to Stephen," I said reluctantly, "but not before I take a few pictures of it."

Jake smiled at me. "That's a good idea. I'll take a few myself, just in case."

"In case of what?"

"You never know. Do you want to know something? It's fun working a case with you, Suzanne."

I nodded in agreement. "I just wish you hadn't agreed to work for Ray first."

"No worries on that count. I've got a hunch we'll do this again someday."

"I'd like that. What should we do now?"

"I don't know about you, but I have a few other leads I need to follow up on," he said as I drove us back home.

"That's the nicest way anyone has ever told me to mind my own business before," I said with a grin.

"Sorry. It's just habit," he admitted.

"I'm just teasing you. I've got to take this to the police, and then I need to bring Grace up to speed on what I've been up to. Dinner tonight?"

"You bet," he said as we got out of the Jeep, since we were back home. I went inside, quickly changed my jeans, and then I rejoined him out front. Before I could drive away, he said, "I know you'll be tempted to stop by Grace's on your way out, but skip her place and go to the police station first, okay?"

"I'll give that some thought," I answered with a grin.

"Wow, I see what you mean."

"About what?" I asked as innocently as I could manage.

"What it's like being blown off by your spouse," he answered with a chuckle as he got into his truck and took off before I could.

Once Jake was gone, I drove straight to Grace's before going to the police station. My husband had been well within his rights to advise me on what to do, but I was a grown woman with a mind of my own, and we both knew that in the end, I was going to do exactly what I wanted to. At the moment, that meant touching base with Grace and showing her what I'd found before turning it over to her boyfriend, the police chief of April Springs.

"How's the paperwork going?" I asked Grace as she answered the door.

"I've done all I can stomach for now," she said with a grin. "Care for something cold to drink?"

"It's a little early for alcohol, isn't it?"

"It's funny that your mind went straight to booze," Grace said with a grin. "I made some fresh lemonade earlier."

"Lemonade in October? Isn't it a bit out of season for that?"

"Is there really a proper season for lemonade?" she asked me. "I wanted some, so I made it. That's one of the perks of being an adult, isn't it?"

"Lemonade it is," I said. "There's something I'd like to ask you."

"Fire away. Whatever it is, the answer is yes," she said as I followed her into the kitchen. Grace had grown up in this house, left to her when her parents had passed away, and what I loved about it most was the fact that it was so close to the cottage where Jake and I now lived. We'd played in the park together as kids, and I was happy that our friendship had survived a bad marriage, untold drama with various men, and even different careers. It was so nice having such a rich history with someone I cared about so much.

"Don't you even want to hear what it is first?"

"I don't need to. I trust that you'll lead me into plenty of mischief, whatever it is you have in mind."

"George has asked us to look into what happened to Tom Thorndike," I said.

"So he doesn't believe it was an accident either, does he?" she asked me as she poured two large glasses of the icy beverage. "Stephen's made up his mind that it was, for some odd reason. I asked him about it at lunch, but he didn't want to talk about it."

"Did you two have lunch together?"

"We often do when we have the time, and I'm in town. Today

we had sandwiches on the back porch. I asked him about his day so far, but he didn't want to talk about it. When I pushed him about Tom, he told me that as far as he was concerned, the case was closed. He's got it in his mind that Tom wasn't averse to taking foolish risks and that he fell of his own accord."

"Why would he think that?" I asked, sincerely curious about it.

"Evidently Tom's phone had all kinds of photos of him doing crazy things like climbing steep cliffs without wearing a harness, whitewater rafting in questionable kayaks, things like that. The last shot on the phone was of Tom standing with his back to the edge of the waterfall and grinning like a maniac. In Stephen's mind, it means that Tom took one step too many, and he paid for it with his life."

"Do you think that's what really happened?"

"I don't know, Suzanne. Have you spoken with Jake about it?"

"He suspects it was foul play, but to be fair, he didn't know about the pictures on Tom's phone, and plus, his mind naturally goes to murder when someone dies. It's an occupational hazard of his former career."

"Is he helping us with the case, too?" she asked me.

"No, he's got his hands full figuring out what Ray Blake did."

"Why doesn't he just ask Ray where he was and what he was up to? That seems as though it would be the simplest way to find out."

"Haven't you heard? Ray got a concussion. He lost somewhere around sixteen hours of his memory, and they might just be crucial ones. Jake will help us if he can, but I've got a feeling that he's not going to be able to do us much good. Is Stephen going to be upset that we're digging into what happened?" I asked her as I took a sip of the lemonade. It was sweet, even for me, and I ran a donut shop.

"I don't think so. He honestly believes it was just an accident, so why would he mind? How about George? Will he help us?"

"We already searched the cottage where Tom was staying together. George owns it, so there was no problem getting in."

She frowned for a second. "I wouldn't mind seeing that for myself."

"Sorry. As we searched, we cleaned the entire place out. There's nothing of value left there now. George wanted it to just be the two of us."

She nodded. "I get that. So, what did you find?"

"Several things, actually. The place had clearly been ransacked, but we still managed to find a few clues. The first thing we stumbled across was a gym pass from Candy's place with a note on the back that said, *Tom, I won't do it, so stop asking.*" I left out the fact that George had missed it and I'd uncovered it later. There was no need to share that particular detail with anyone else.

"That's kind of cryptic. What did she say when you asked her about it?"

"I haven't spoken with her yet. I was saving that particular conversation for the two of us," I told Grace with a grin.

"Excellent. You know me. I'm always up for a face to face with Candy," she answered in kind. "What else did you find?"

"Ray's business card, torn up and in the trash. On the back, it said, "*We Need To Talk,*" and it appears that Tom wasn't at all interested in making that happen."

"Too bad we can't ask him about it," she said. "Is that it?"

"No. George also found a thousand dollars in the oatmeal canister."

"There's no reason to be sarcastic, Suzanne. I was just curious."

"It's the truth," I said. "There was a thin tube of money hidden inside the oatmeal container."

"Wow, and to think I keep my money in the bank," she said.

"We both figured he had a lot more than that, but if it was in that cottage, we didn't find it, and we turned the place upside down. I've got a feeling that somewhere in this town is a load of cash just waiting to be found."

"Did you take photos of any of this?" she asked me.

"Yes, but I did better than that. I've got both the torn-up business card and the gym pass out in the Jeep."

"Where's the cash? Is it out there, too?"

"George is holding on to it," I said. We hadn't even discussed it, but since he'd found it, I didn't have any problem with him taking charge of it. I had no idea what he'd do with it, but I trusted him, not just with a thousand dollars but with my life.

"Of course he is," Grace said with a grin. "It couldn't be in safer hands, and if you left it out in your Jeep and someone stole it, nobody would be happy. So do we suspect Ray in all of this, or does he get a free pass?"

"Why, because he's Emma's father and Sharon's husband? I don't see how we can strike his name because of that. He has to be on our list, but we should let Jake handle that part of the investigation, since it overlaps with ours."

"That sounds solid. Who else do we suspect?"

"Candy has to be on our list until we figure out how she's involved in this. Mitchell Bloom is on it, too."

"Why Mitchell?"

"He was in the donut shop flashing a wad of bills around, and he even bought everyone donuts with a fifty-dollar bill."

Grace frowned at me. "I agree that it's out of character, but does he deserve our scrutiny because of some eccentric behavior?"

"There's also the fact that Trish overheard him arguing with Tom about money not long before he died," I told her.

"My, you've been busy without me, haven't you?" Grace asked, smiling.

"Some of it I found out on my own, and the rest just seemed to fall into my lap."

"Either way, we've got a good start."

"There's one more suspect, at least I think he might be," I said. "A stranger approached me about buying the donut shop, but I didn't believe him."

"Okay. And that connects to Tom how exactly?"

"He asked me about Tom as nonchalantly as he could manage, even pretending to forget his name, but the harder he tried to act casual about his questioning, the more alarmed I got. The man bears watching."

"You didn't happen to catch his name, did you?"

"He said it was Daryl Lane, but whether that's the truth or not, I have no way of knowing," I said.

"So we need to look into him as well. It's a good thing you asked me for my help. You've been stirring up so much buzz around town, you need someone to watch your back."

"Thanks for being there for me."

"Suzanne, there's nothing in the world I'd rather be doing, and you know it." Grace gestured to the dining room table, covered in paperwork. "I've got the rest of the week to wade through all of this, and I don't have any other responsibilities until I do, so count me in."

"Wonderful," I said as I finished drinking the lemonade. Funny. It had started out much too sweet for me, but by the time I'd emptied my glass, it had tasted just right to me.

"Then let's get started."

"Oh, I nearly forgot. We have to make one stop before we start digging," I added.

"I can't wait to hear where we're going that's so important it takes precedence over our investigation."

I pulled the baggied button and cloth from my fresh jeans and held it out to her. "I found this on the path coming down from the falls when Jake and I went up to investigate. He insisted that I turn it over to Stephen immediately, but I wanted you to see it first."

She took it from me, studied it from all angles, snapped a few photos of it with her phone as well, and then she handed it back to me. "It's probably nothing. You know that, don't you?"

"Maybe, but Jake was insistent that I share it with the chief, and I think he was right. I don't want to conceal evidence from the police, even if they don't believe there was a crime."

"Good girl," Grace said as she stood and grabbed her jacket. "Let's go see my boyfriend and hear what he has to say."

CHAPTER 15

"WHAT'S THIS?" STEPHEN GRANT ASKED as I put the button and cloth remnant down on his desktop. The police chief had been doing paperwork when Grace and I had asked to see him, and he'd been almost pitifully delighted to be distracted from it.

"I found it just off the hiking trail coming down from Laurel Falls this afternoon," I said.

Chief Grant picked it up, and then, instead of studying the contents, he examined the baggie it had come in. "Since when did you start carrying around evidence bags with you?"

"Jake was with me," I said. "Have you heard about the stranger in town asking around about Tom Thorndike?"

"I heard something about it," he acknowledged. "That's about all that I've heard about him, though. A name would be helpful."

"It's Daryl Lane," I supplied.

The chief looked startled by my revelation. "How do you happen to know that?"

"He pretended to ask about buying the donut shop, but it was pretty clear that what he really wanted to talk about was Tom."

"Hang on a second," the chief said, and then he tapped a few words into his computer. After a moment, he frowned. "Suzanne, are you sure about that name?"

"That's what he told me it was. Why? Did you get any hits?"

"He was in prison around the same time Tom was being held, and he's apparently a pretty bad apple."

"What did he do?" Grace asked him.

"Let's see. Assault with a deadly weapon, extortion, arson, and those are just the highlights. Regardless of why he's really in town, if you talk to him again, let me know immediately, okay?"

"You've got it," I said.

"I mean it, Suzanne. He's not someone you should be messing around with."

"Believe me, I don't have any desire to get him angry at me. I'll let you know if I see him again."

That seemed to satisfy the police chief. "Your husband doesn't think Tom Thorndike was murdered too, does he?" Stephen asked.

"He's not ruling it out, but then again, he doesn't know everything you do about the case."

The chief looked at Grace for a moment before speaking. "Did you tell her about the photos we found on Tom's phone?"

"Was I not supposed to? I'm sorry; I thought she might like to know. If I was wrong to say anything, I apologize."

He chewed it over for a second before replying. "No, it's okay." Turning back to me, he said, "Suzanne, it appeared that Tom was quite the adventurer. I found two dozen photos on his cell phone of him in some pretty precarious places. The waterfall shot was one of the milder ones, to be honest with you. If you were just at the top of the falls, you must have noticed how slippery those rocks were."

"They weren't that bad," I said.

"Maybe not, but I'm guessing you didn't climb on them with your back turned toward the edge so you could take a picture of yourself. What possesses people to do that?"

"It helps them share their lives with their friends on social media," Grace said. "There's nothing wrong with it, unless it's taken to extremes."

"Like this time," the chief said as he pushed the button and cloth segment back at me. "Where exactly on the trail did you find that?"

"My feet went out from under me, and I slipped off the path," I admitted, even though it made me look quite a bit clumsier than I really was. "This was on the ground right by my hand, and it's easy to see how someone else slipped just like I did. Jake said that Ray's clothes were intact, so it didn't come from the clothes he was wearing."

That got the police chief's attention. "How does Jake happen to know that for a fact?"

"You need to ask him," I said. I knew it wasn't my place to share my husband's new task with the chief of police.

"I will, but right now I'm asking you."

"Just call him," I said.

Chief Grant clouded up. "I can't imagine what's so secret that you can't tell me yourself."

"Oh, for goodness sakes, Suzanne, just tell him." She turned to her boyfriend and said, "Ray has asked Jake to look into where he was during the time he can't remember."

"Grace, that wasn't your information to share," I told her.

Instead of looking remorseful, she simply shrugged. "I told you about the photos on Tom's phone, so I thought Stephen deserved something as well. He was going to find out sooner or later anyway, so why not tell him now?"

I tried to be upset with her, but in a way, she'd done me a favor. At least I hadn't been the one to divulge Jake's new job, and if my husband was going to be cross with someone, all in all, I rather wanted it to be with someone besides me. "I suppose you're right."

"See, that's why you both need me around," she said with a grin. "I'm an excellent communication facilitator."

"Is that what you call it?" the chief asked her. "Listen, I appreciate you bringing this by my office, but I'm not exactly sure what it means." He frowned for a moment before asking, "Did Jake suggest that you bring this to me?"

"He might have," I said, hedging my bets. I couldn't tell if Stephen was happy or displeased about the prospect, so I wasn't going to commit either way until I had a better idea of why he was asking me the question.

"There's no need to answer. I know that he did," Stephen said with a smile. "Once a cop, always a cop. Thank him for me, okay?"

It was a clear dismissal, but I wasn't ready to go yet. "What do you think really happened to Ray Blake, Chief?"

The police chief shrugged. "He most likely tripped and hit his head on something. I've got a feeling that ten or twelve of those missing hours were spent unconscious. When he woke up, he was still disoriented, and that's why they found him wandering around on the road. I'm not exactly sure what Jake is supposed to do about it, and I don't envy him the task of tracking down Ray's movements, but hey, he's welcome to try. Now, if you two will excuse me, I've got to get to this mound of paperwork before five, or I won't be by for dinner tonight, Grace."

She leaned forward and gave him a quick kiss. "Are we good?"

"As gold," he said with a smile. "Now skedaddle."

"Yes, sir. You bet, Mr. Police Chief."

Stephen Grant laughed as we were leaving, and once we were back outside of the police station, Grace turned to me and asked, "Are we okay as well?"

"Sure. I wasn't happy about you telling Stephen what Jake was up to, but at least I didn't have to do it myself."

"Stephen was starting to steam up, Suzanne. I knew if I

didn't say something quickly, it might end up being blown up into something worse than it was, so I took the plunge. Tell Jake I'm sorry if he's bothered by it."

"You could always tell him yourself," I suggested with a smile.

"No, thanks. I'll leave that up to you. Now, despite what my boyfriend believes, I'm getting the distinct impression that we're not just giving up and going home. Is that right?"

"The police chief makes a good point, but George asked us to look into this, and until he's satisfied that it was an accident, I say we keep digging."

"I'm game if you are," she said. "Where do we start?"

"It's got to be Candy Murphy," I said.

"Why does it have to be her?" Grace asked me.

"Because if we don't talk to her first, I'll just keep putting it off as long as I can."

"You aren't a big fan of Candy's, are you?"

"It's not that. Well, at least it's not *just* that," I admitted. "I've long suspected that she's quite a bit smarter than she lets on. This ditzy act may just be a disguise hiding something deeper."

"Do you think that's possible?" Grace asked me. "She's always seemed like a complete airhead to me, an empty box covered in pretty wrapping paper."

"I thought so too for the longest time, but over the past few years, I haven't been quite so sure."

"Well, if she's acting dumb, the girl deserves an Oscar. She could give Max lessons."

"Not that he'd take them, at least not now. Back when he was constantly on the prowl, Candy would have been his perfect type, but ever since he got involved with Emily Hargraves, I don't think he's strayed even once."

"Speaking of Emily, have you been by her newsstand lately?"

Our friend owned and operated her own newsstand, named Two Cows And A Moose after her three childhood stuffed animals, who were all displayed prominently in her shop, usually wearing custom outfits she'd created for them. "No, what are the guys dressed up as now?"

"Well, with Halloween coming soon, she's got them all in costume again ready to go trick-or-treating."

I laughed to myself, remembering some of the crazy things she'd put them in during past years. "What did she pick this year?"

"She swears it was their choice. She made one costume that takes all three of them to fill up, and then some. Their legs are all poking out of a monstrously huge octopus costume, with two fake legs sewn on for good measure so they equal eight. The funniest part is that she's got their little faces poking out in various places on the costume. They are each wearing masks she's fashioned out of cloth seashells, and their faces are pretty easily recognizable."

"I thought Cow and Spots were identical," I said. "How can you tell them apart?"

"She got Spots first, so she hugged him so hard that his face is narrower and leaner than Cow's is. You knew that, right?"

"Of course," I said, doing my best to keep a straight face. Emily acted as though her three stuffed animals were alive, much like Hobbes from the cartoon *Calvin and Hobbes*, and anyone who spent much time around them found themselves being sucked into the mythos as well. I knew for a fact that last Christmas, which was the time of year Emily first got them as a child, Max had delivered birthday presents to each of them. He had some bone-shaped graham cracker treats added to little hand-painted buckets, two of which read "Cow Treats" while the third said "Moose Treats." That gesture, as well as many more, told me that he loved Emily on a level that he had never come close to loving me. I didn't resent it, though. In fact, I enjoyed seeing him grow into a level of commitment and maturity that I'd never suspected he could reach. Then again, I might have been able to be happy for them since I'd found the love of my life myself. "I'll have to go check them out."

"You really should," she said. "So, do we come up with a cover story for Candy, or do we just come out and ask her about the note she gave Tom?"

"I'm not sure. What do you think?" I asked as I drove us to Candy's gym. It had gone through rough times since she'd lost her older, and married, boyfriend's sponsorship, but somehow she'd managed to keep her business afloat when many others failed.

"I would have said we couldn't be too subtle before, but since you think there's a crafty fox hiding in there, maybe we should be a little less direct than usual."

"Then again, we don't want to blow her cover if she is indeed hiding the fact that she's actually pretty smart. Let's start by playing along with her ruse and see where that gets us."

"You're the boss. I'm just the hired hand."

"You're more than that, and you know it," I told her.

"Hey, I wasn't complaining. I get enough of being a boss on my regular job. It's kind of nice to be able to sit back and let you take over our investigations."

"But you'll chime in if you think I'm missing something, right?" I asked her with a smile.

Her grin was wide and happy. "Do you even have to ask me that question?"

We pulled up in front of Candy's gym, and I was happy to see that there were only a few cars there at the moment. Hopefully she wouldn't be able to avoid us, and we could get her undivided attention.

Taking a deep breath, I put my hand on the door of the gym and walked inside with Grace on my heels.

The gym had changed since I'd been there last. Gone were the frilly decorations, the juice bar, and many of the other amenities. Now it looked more like a place to work out instead of socialize.

"I love what you've done to the place," I told Candy when she greeted us.

"Is that sarcasm, Suzanne?" she asked. Candy was wearing yoga pants that left nothing to the imagination, a sports bra that was revealing as well, and an oversized man's shirt that looked as though it had seen better days. I had to give her credit for one thing; if it was possible, Candy looked even better than she had in high school, which was no small accomplishment.

"Actually, I'm quite serious," I said. "It looks like a real gym now."

"Well, I had to scale back on a few things when I lost my sponsorship." What she'd really lost was her married boyfriend, but I wasn't there to quibble about that. Leonard Branch had gone back to his wife and left Candy on her own. Instead of falling flat on her face, she'd risen to the challenge and had found a way to keep afloat, which was a type of success in and of itself. "I'm proud of what I've accomplished here. I'd like to think that I'm capable of changing, you know?"

I suddenly realized that she was right. Though she still dressed provocatively, the ditzy Candy was gone, and the savvy one I'd spotted only glimpses of in the past was out in full force. I realized instantly that it changed the way I needed to approach her. "I think you've done well, too."

She took the compliment in stride. "I'm wagering you two aren't here about a gym membership. What can I do for you?"

Grace was about to speak when I beat her to it, which was a change of pace for us. "We'd like to ask you about this," I said as I pulled out the pass, as well as the note, from my jeans and handed it to her. Grace looked surprised by my action for a moment, but she quickly hid it. I caught that out of the corner of my eye, but most of my focus was on Candy. How she reacted to the note was just as important as what she might say next.

She took it from me, still in the evidence baggie I'd gotten from Jake's stash. Candy shrugged when she saw the pass. "I hand these out now and then. It's no big deal. Would you each like one?" she asked as she pulled a handful out of a drawer at the check-in desk.

"Flip it over," I told her.

Candy did as I asked, and the moment she saw the message, she frowned.

"Did you write that note?" I asked her.

"You know that I did," she said. "Where did you find this?"

"It was at Tom Thorndike's cottage," I replied. "What does it mean?"

"It's personal," Candy said, but I noticed that she still held on to the pass.

"May I have that back, please?"

She didn't do as I asked, though. "What possible use could you have for this? It was between Tom and me and no one else."

"But Tom is dead, and this could be part of a police investigation," I said. Both facts were true, and even though the police weren't investigating Tom's death, that didn't mean that they wouldn't if we were able to come up with some concrete evidence and a scenario that might discredit the police chief's theory that Tom's death had been accidental.

"I didn't kill him," she said. "I thought he fell."

"It has yet to be determined if he fell or if he was pushed," Grace chimed in.

Candy took that in. "I don't have any desire to air my dirty laundry with the two of you. This," she said as she tapped the note, "was between us. It's no one else's business. As a matter of fact, I'm going to keep it." She clutched the pass and its note in her hands, defying us to challenge her.

"No worries. We've got copies, and photographs of it as well," I said. I'd made a mistake not showing her a copy instead of the actual item, but I was going to pretend that it didn't matter. It had been sloppy work though, and I chided myself for not being more careful with what might turn out to be a crucial piece of evidence. "If I were you, I'd take very good care of that if you really mean to keep it. If it were to be accidentally destroyed or lost, the police would take a very dim view of it, and you wouldn't want them digging into your life any more than they had to, would you?"

Candy gave that a moment's thought, and then she flung the pass and note back to me. "Fine. You keep it. I don't care."

"If that's the truth, then tell us what it meant," I said. "What was Tom asking you to do, and why were you so reluctant to do it?"

Candy scowled openly at me. "What possible business is it of yours, Suzanne?"

"Important people in this town want to know what happened to Tom Thorndike," I said. "If we report back that you were exonerated, it would serve you well. If we have to say that you weren't cooperative, it might mean more scrutiny than you're ready for." I'd been purposefully vague, hoping that Candy would fill in the blanks with her own demons.

"He wanted me to sleep with him, okay?" she finally admitted. "I spurned his advances, but he wouldn't take no for an answer. There, are you satisfied?"

It didn't sound like Tom to me, but then again, did I really know the man he'd become from the boy I'd once dated so long ago? "Did anyone else witness any of these advances?" I asked her.

"Not that I'm aware of. He was very careful to make sure that no one else was around when he made his passes at me." That worked out neatly for her, but I wasn't at all sure that I trusted her.

"Why should we believe you?" Grace asked her.

"I'm not at all sure that I care," she said. "Now, I have a training session in ten minutes, and I have to get ready for it, if you'll excuse me."

"Sure thing," I said. "You don't mind if we come back later, do you?"

"Why would you need to?" Candy asked me, clearly unhappy about the request.

"We have several more people to speak with," Grace said. "New information has a way of coming to light, and there might be some things we need clarified."

Before Candy could respond, Grace and I headed to the door, bumping into a pudgy man wearing entirely too much spandex. "I'm ready for my session, Candy," he said happily.

"Go get warmed up, and I'll be right with you," Candy said, and then she turned to us and said, "Good bye."

At that point, we really didn't have much choice but to leave.

"Do you believe Candy?" I asked Grace once we were outside.

"I'm not sure. Can you imagine Tom pursuing her?" she asked me.

"Actually, that part didn't surprise me. She's pretty in a flashy kind of way, and Tom always seemed to prefer that type. He had a crush on her back in high school. Why wouldn't he try to date her now? What I'm having trouble believing is that he'd pursue her so relentlessly that she felt the need to send him a note telling him to stop."

"If she's lying to us about that, then what did that note really mean?" Grace asked me.

"I wish I knew, but we don't have enough information yet. She's changed, though; that much is for sure. Did you notice?"

"You were right. She's smarter than I would have ever given her credit for. That makes her dangerous in my mind."

"Why do you say that?" I asked Grace.

"If she's showing us her real side, it could be a warning to us not to mess with her. Nice finesse with the note, by the way. I wasn't sure we'd ever get that back once it left your hands."

"I really messed up showing her the original," I agreed. "I won't make that mistake again. Before we speak with anyone else, we need to make copies of all of our evidence and put the originals away someplace safely."

"I've got a safe at home, and a color copier, too," Grace volunteered. "Let's go take care of that before we tackle Mitchell Bloom."

"I'm really not sure how to approach him," I said. "I'd rather not tell him that Trish overheard him fighting with Tom about money in the park."

"You could always claim that you overheard it yourself," Grace said as we headed for her place.

"What good would that do?"

"Well, you've already got a target on your back since you're investigating what happened to Tom. Could it really hurt to claim that you were the one who overheard them talking? I could do it myself, for that matter. My house is nearly as close to the park as yours. I can claim that I was taking a walk and overheard everything."

"No, I'll do it," I said. I wasn't about to let Grace put herself in any more danger than I had to. I'd made that mistake once with George when he'd been helping me with an investigation, and it had cost him dearly, something that I never wanted to repeat. "It makes more sense, since my place is even closer."

"Are you sure?"

"Positive," I said. "Now, let's get these copies made so we can tackle the next name on our list."

It took all of ten minutes to do everything we wanted to at Grace's place, and that included backing up the images from our phones to the cloud using her computer. Now, if we lost the originals, we'd at least have backups of everything. I wasn't a huge fan of society's overreliance on technology, including communication, but sometimes it could be a good thing. With copies of everything we needed in our hands, we were ready to approach Mitchell Bloom about his argument and his newfound wealth.

CHAPTER 16

"**M**ITCHELL, DO YOU HAVE A second?" I asked when we walked into the auto-supply store where he worked. It was one of the few chains that had made its way to April Springs, and it had made me uneasy since it had first opened. We'd so far mostly escaped the encroachment of the chain-store mentality the rest of the country seemed so wrapped up in. Our town was just too small for most of them to bother with, and to go to one of the large big-box stores, we had to drive thirty minutes or more, which was fine by me. I was the main source of donuts in town, and folks seemed to love what I offered, but I wasn't under any delusions that I could stand up under direct competition from Krispy Kreme or Dunkin Donuts. I might even produce better donuts than either one of them managed on their massive scales, but I wasn't in any hurry to find out if my business model would be sustainable under a direct attack from nationwide competition.

"Did something happen to your Jeep?" he asked, and I realized that it was a perfect opening. If I could get him to help me with my vehicle, maybe Grace and I could question him without coming right out and accusing him of anything.

"The wipers are getting old," I said, something that Jake had commented on more than a few times lately during heavy rain.

"We can take care of that," he said with a grin. "What year is your Jeep?"

"I have no idea," I admitted. "Should I know that?"

"We can find out easily enough," he said, and then he called out to another man at the counter. "I'll be back in a second, Harry."

The man waved a distracted hand in the air as he studied a partially dismantled engine part sitting on his counter. It could have been anything as far as I was concerned, since I wasn't exactly a mechanic.

As the three of us walked out to the Jeep, he asked, "Could I see your registration?"

"Why? It doesn't need to be inspected," I told him.

"It's got the year, make, and model printed on it," Mitchell explained.

"Oh," I said as I retrieved it and handed it to him. "Folks are still talking about your kindness buying donuts for everyone this morning, Mitchell." Had it really just been today that Ray had been found and Tom's body had been discovered? A lot had happened since then, that was for sure.

"I kind of got carried away in the heat of the moment," he said sheepishly. "I probably shouldn't have done that."

"It must take you a while to make fifty dollars working here," I said, and then I quickly added, "I know it takes me quite a bit of time to accumulate that much."

"I won a lot more than that in a poker game the other night," Mitchell said absently. "I believe I've got those wiper blades in stock. Follow me."

I wasn't eager to grill him inside with other witnesses. "Can you install them for me, too?"

"Sure, and free of charge, too. It's what we do," he said.

Once we were at the display back in the store, I saw a selection of wipers that boggled my mind. Not only were there several different brands, but the sizes were staggering as well. "How am I supposed to choose?"

"It's not as complicated as it looks," he said. "Do you want coach or first class?"

I thought about the low net worth of my Jeep. "Coach," I said decisively.

He grinned. "Got it. Now, do you want the cheapest, the middle, or the high end in the coach range?"

"Let's shoot for the middle," I answered.

"Good choice." Once he looked up my Jeep's specs, he got two wipers and headed back outside.

"About that poker game," I said. "Who else was playing? My husband, Jake, is always looking for a game." That was a total and complete fabrication, but I figured Mitchell wouldn't know that.

"It was over in Union Square," he said absently.

"Can you be more specific than that?" He just shrugged in reply, so as he started pulling off one of my old wipers, I added, "I thought you might have gotten that money from Tom Thorndike."

The old wiper arm snapped in his hands.

"Did you just break my Jeep?" I asked him incredulously.

"No worries, it's all part of the blade assembly," he said as nonchalantly as possible. "What makes you think I got any money from Tom?"

"I wasn't eavesdropping or anything, but I was taking a walk in the park since my cottage is right there, and I heard you two arguing about money the other night."

Mitchell frowned as he finished installing one blade and got started on the other. "I floated him a few bucks during the game, and he hadn't paid me back yet. It was nothing."

"If it was nothing, then why did you sound so angry with him?" I asked, pushing him a little harder. "You must have been really upset."

"I'm telling you, it wasn't that big a deal," he said, though according to Trish, it had been pretty heated. "He paid me back, and that's all there was to it." Mitchell took both spent blades and said, "Finished. Let's go inside and settle up."

He rang the sale up on his register, and I tried to hide my astonishment at the cost of new wiper blades. Still, I had needed them, and at least I hadn't gone for the first-class model.

"Was that the last time you saw Tom?" Grace asked him.

"I thought he slipped and fell," Mitchell said a little testily. "Why all the questions?"

"We're just curious, I guess," I said.

"Well, be careful. You know what happened to the cat."

Grace asked him levelly, "Mitchell, was that a threat?"

"What? No! Of course not. Listen, I've got a shipment in back to unpack. I hope you enjoy your new wiper blades, Suzanne."

"I don't believe him for one second," I said once we were outside. "Do you?"

"I don't know. It sounds plausible," Grace replied.

"It's a little *too* pat, don't you think? He's hiding something."

"Are you sure you're not just jumping at shadows?" Grace asked me as I started driving back to her place. I still wanted to speak with Daryl Lane, but at this point, I had no idea how to find him, and it was getting late. Jake would be home soon, and I was worn out from my extraordinarily busy day.

"Maybe I am," I said. "Should we take this up tomorrow? I should be free after eleven-thirty."

"That sounds good to me. I'll come by the donut shop and pick you up," Grace offered.

"Why don't I pick *you* up after I go home, take a shower, and change?"

"It sounds like a plan to me. Don't worry, Suzanne. We're making progress."

"Funny, but it doesn't feel like it, does it?"

"These things take time," Grace answered. "I don't have to tell you that."

"No, you don't."

Once I dropped her off at home, I drove the last few hundred feet to the cottage, and I was pleasantly surprised to see Jake's truck already parked out front.

I didn't go inside at once though. As I neared my front door, I heard someone crying in the park nearby.

Jake could wait.

Someone was hurting, and if I could help them at all, then I would.

"Jennifer, is that you?" I found one of Emma's friends sitting on a nearby park bench trying her best to staunch her flow of tears.

"Mrs. Hart. Hi," she said as she tried to hide the fact that she'd been crying.

"Please, call me Suzanne. What happened?" Jennifer had always been cute, a pleasantly plump redhead with freckles across her nose and an energy that had always impressed me. It was absent now for the first time since I'd known her.

"It's my boyfriend. At least he used to be my boyfriend."

A sudden chill went through me. "His name wasn't Tom by any chance, was it?" It would be just like Tom Thorndike to go after a girl like this. If she was twenty years old, she hadn't gotten there very long ago, and she had a sweet innocence about her, accompanied by a pleasing figure, that would be right up his alley.

"No, his name was Kyle, and he just dumped me for Brenda Cramer. He said she was his soul mate, but I know it's got nothing to do with her soul. I don't even know why I'm so upset. Kyle was a terrible boyfriend, and I've had more than my share of them. Can you believe it? He dumped me with a text message," she lamented, and then she started crying again. I sat down and put my arm around her, and as I did, I tried my best to soothe her.

"He sounds like a real loser," I said. "Are you sure you're not better off without him?"

"That's easy for you to say. You've got someone special in your life."

"Jake? Yes, I do. Jennifer, did you know that I was married before?"

She stopped crying for a second as she looked at me. "Really?"

"There's no reason you'd know it, but I spent some time being wed to Max Thornburg."

"The actor? He's really handsome, isn't he?" she asked, as though I wasn't well aware of the fact of my ex's good looks.

"Yes, but it was a terrible marriage that ended badly. Max wasn't the only frog I kissed before I found my prince, if you know what I mean."

"All I seem to get are toads," she said. "Lee says it's because I'm too trusting."

"Who's Lee?" I asked her.

Her face cleared up for a moment. "He's a guy I went to school with. Emma knows him. We've been friends for a long time. I wish I could find a guy like him."

"Is he married?"

"What? No."

"Does he have a girlfriend?" I asked.

"Not really. He can't seem to find anybody, either. I don't know why. He's kind, he's smart, he's funny, and he never breaks his word. He's a really special guy."

I'd seen it before. I had a hunch that Lee was smitten with

her but was too shy to do anything about it. "Have you ever considered asking *him* out?"

"You mean like on a date?" she asked me incredulously.

"That's exactly what I mean. Jennifer, it's entirely possible that he's got a crush on you, but he's too shy to do anything about it. Would it be the worst thing in the world if you asked him out? I'll bet you a dollar to a dozen donuts he'd jump at the chance to go out on a date with you."

"Lee and I? I never even considered it," she said slowly, but I noticed that her tears were drying up even as she contemplated the idea. "What if he says no? I'll make a fool of myself."

"Maybe, but what if he says yes? What are you looking for in a boyfriend? Does Lee have those qualities?"

She thought about it for a few moments and then nodded. "Yes."

"Do you find him attractive?" I asked her. That was important as well, though it wasn't everything by any stretch of the imagination.

"Yes, I've always thought he was cute."

"Then ask him out," I said. "Kyle doesn't seem all that worthy of your tears. Isn't it time you took a chance on someone who might be exactly what you need?"

"I'm not sure if I'm brave enough," Jennifer said in a soft voice.

"You can do it," I said. "I have faith in you."

"Maybe you're right," she said. "I need to think about it a little bit, though."

"Well, at the very least, it will stop you from thinking about Kyle."

"Thanks, Mrs. Hart, I mean Suzanne. Emma was right about you."

It surprised me that my assistant had discussed me with anyone else. "About what?"

"She said that you were kind and smart, and that not only were you a great boss, but you were an even better friend," Jennifer said. "I shouldn't have told you that."

"Why on earth not?" I asked, suddenly feeling my own load lighten a little. I had nothing but warm feelings for Emma, and it was nice hearing that she felt the same way about me. That was saying something, too, considering how closely we worked together. "How are you feeling now?"

"Better," she said. "I'm going to walk home, work up my courage, and then I'm going to call Lee before I lose my nerve."

"I hope you'll be pleasantly surprised, but even if you're not, you should be proud of yourself for taking your fate into your own hands. Good luck."

As we both stood, she hugged me tightly. "Thank you."

"I'm glad I could help," I said.

As she walked away, I marveled at how complex life could be for a young woman her age. Her emotions ran strong, but she was a fine young lady, and if it was what she truly wanted, I hoped that she'd be lucky enough to find someone worthy of her love. Either way, she was taking responsibility for her life, and that could make her nothing but stronger as far as I was concerned. I turned back to the cottage to join Jake, happy yet again that I'd found him. There was nothing that gave me more appreciation that he was there waiting for me than to be reminded about the times I'd spent crying in the park myself over the years before he'd finally found his way into my life.

CHAPTER 17

"HEY, SUZANNE. I THOUGHT I heard you drive up ten minutes ago," my husband said as I walked into our cottage.

"I did, but I had a mission of mercy to run first," I said as I kissed him enthusiastically.

After we broke off, he stepped back and smiled. "Hey, are you okay?"

"I'm fine," I said happily.

"Not that I'm complaining, but what was with that kiss? It was a little more enthusiastic than I usually get."

"I'm just really happy that we found each other," I said.

"I won't argue with that. So, what exactly was your mission?" he asked me.

"I suppose you could say that I ran into a ghost of bad boyfriend past," I said. "It's a modern girl's version of Dickens."

Jake looked puzzled. "Is that supposed to make any sense?"

"No," I said with a laugh. "Are you hungry? I'd be glad to whip something up."

"Actually, I was hoping you'd go somewhere with me," he said.

"Sure. Let's go," I said, keeping my coat on.

"Don't you even want to know where we're going?"

"Jake, if you're going to be there, that's all I need to know."

"I appreciate your trust in me, but you might not like it."

"Try me," I said.

"Ray Blake wants to see you at the hospital," Jake said.

"Why on earth would he want to see me?" I asked my husband.

"For some reason, he thinks you might be the key in his missing timeline," Jake explained.

"I can't imagine how that could be true. I didn't see him the entire time he was missing." What an odd thing for Ray to think. I loved his wife and daughter dearly. As to the newspaperman himself, I could take him or leave him, though he had been showing signs of personal growth over the past couple of years. When Emma had first started working for me at Donut Hearts, Ray had treated her as though she were nine years old, even though she had been twice that age. Over the past few years, though, he'd grown to treat her more and more like the adult she really was, though he inevitably had a lapse every now and then.

"I told him you would have said something to me if you had seen him, but he won't listen to reason. I'm supposed to ask you to indulge him, if you wouldn't mind."

"Did Emma put you up to it?"

"Yes, but mostly it was Sharon," he said. "She's worried about her husband. I know they have an odd relationship, but it seems to work for them."

"Hey, I've learned never to try to judge someone else's marriage," I said. "Let's go."

"Should we grab something along the way?" Jake asked me. "I could throw together a couple of sandwiches for the road."

"Let's see what the hospital cafeteria has," I suggested. "I'm not about to face Ray Blake on an empty stomach."

"Are you sure that's where you want to eat?" my husband asked with a frown.

"Haven't you heard? They hired some kid from a culinary school in Georgia. He's supposed to be fantastic."

"If you say so," Jake said. "I'll have to taste it myself to believe it."

"Then let's give it a shot."

After he put down his fork, Jake said, "I never could have imagined something this good came from a hospital cafeteria. This pasta and chicken is unbelievable."

"I know," I said, spearing the last bit of cream-covered pasta with my fork and popping it into my mouth. "It's pretty amazing."

An older woman wearing the hospital's generic smock came by collecting trays that folks had left on their tables. As a lark, I said, "Please give our compliments to the chef."

She grinned broadly at us. "I'll tell Barton that you enjoyed your meal. He's really something, isn't he? I'm going to miss him terribly."

"Miss him? Where is he going?" Jake asked, suddenly having a personal stake in the new culinary expert in town.

"He got an offer for twice as much money to run a restaurant in Charlotte. Funny thing is, if the owner hadn't gotten food poisoning and come here, he never would have found Barton. I know it's a wonderful opportunity for him, but man oh man, I wish that fellow had gotten sick somewhere else."

"I second the motion," Jake said.

"Is there any of this left?" I asked her.

"There's quite a bit, actually," she said. "He got carried away and made way too much of it. Do you want seconds?"

I couldn't dream of eating another bite, but I had a different idea. "Have him make up four containers of this to go, and we'll pick them up on our way out. We're here visiting someone, but this is too good to just experience once."

"I'll tell him," she said, and then she turned around as a kid barely out of short pants approached us, wearing the full chef's regalia.

"Barton, do you have a second? These folks want to talk to you about your food."

The young man frowned. "I used too much thyme again,

didn't I?" he asked with a scowl. "It's tough getting the ingredients just right on the kind of scale I'm cooking on. I apologize."

Jake stood and stuck out his hand. "Sir, that was one of the best meals I've ever had in my life." He then turned to me and added, "No offense, Suzanne."

"None taken," I said as I stood as well. "I agree with you. We're going to miss you, and we've only just met."

He smiled happily. "I'm getting my own kitchen. Six weeks out of school and my dreams are already coming true. I'm glad you enjoyed your meal."

"We love it so much we're getting some to take home. I would think that it would freeze well. Am I right?"

"I like to serve it fresh, but it should be nearly as good frozen," the young man said with a only a hint of displeasure.

"Nearly as good is better than anything I can make fresh," I said with a laugh. "I only wish my donuts tasted half this good."

His face lit up. "I knew you looked familiar. You run Donut Hearts, don't you? I had a Kool-Aid donut that was amazing. How do you do it?"

"If you're in town long enough, come by the shop around three AM sometime and I'll show you," I said, joking.

"I'd be delighted. I'm not even in bed by then on most nights."

"It's a date, then," I said.

Jake grinned happily as he paid for our meals, and the ones we would be coming back for as well. "I told you that your donuts were great," my husband said happily. "You've got a trained chef asking about your recipe."

"I'm sure it was just out of politeness."

"I saw his face, Suzanne. He was sincere. Now I have a hankering for one of those Kool-Aid donuts. You don't have any left over, do you?"

I had to laugh. "You know I don't keep any treats overnight, but I'll be glad to save you a few tomorrow."

"It's a deal," he said. "Well, we've put it off as long as we could. Are you ready to see Ray?"

"I am, though I'm not at all sure what good it will do."

"Let's go find out."

We found Emma and Sharon coming out of the designated room as we started to knock on Ray's door. "Is everything okay?" I asked them.

Emma hugged me. "Suzanne! Thanks so much for coming. He's insisting that he talk to you, but he won't tell us why. Do you have any idea what he's after?"

"No, I'm just as confused as you are," I said. I turned to Sharon and asked her, "How are you doing?"

"I'm just happy he's okay," she said. "When we couldn't find him, I figured I'd never see him again. I couldn't stand it."

"But you did," I said. "Ladies, we'll stay with Ray until you get back. Have you two eaten yet?"

"No, we didn't want to leave Dad alone," Emma said.

"Then you need to go down to the cafeteria this second and order the chicken and pasta special. It's got some kind of white sauce, and something else I can't put my finger on, that is incredibly good," I told them.

"I've heard about the food here. It's supposed to be really good," Sharon said.

"Trust me, you'll want to experience it for yourself while you still can. Go on. Now shoo. We've got this."

The women looked at me, each in turn, and nodded as they silently thanked me for coming. Sharon paused before leaving. "You'll call us if there's any change, won't you?"

"I promise," I said.

"I may never leave home again," she replied quietly. One of the reasons Sharon liked helping Emma out at the donut shop when it was her turn to run it was so that she could finance trips abroad with her girlfriends. Ray was a notorious homebody, afraid to leave his newspaper in anyone else's hands, so Sharon had decided to see the world without him.

"I hope that's not true," I said. "You've gotten so much joy out of traveling over the years."

"I know, but what if this had happened while I was in Athens or Madrid? I would have been half a world away when he needed me most."

"We can't live our lives worrying about what tomorrow might bring," I told her. "Go eat." In a softer voice, I added, "Emma looks as though she could use a break." I knew that appealing to her maternal instincts was the best way to get her to focus on the here and now.

"Of course."

"Well played," Jake said softly before we went into Ray Blake's room.

"I don't know what you're talking about," I answered him with a grin.

Ray was sitting up in bed staring off into space when we entered the sterile white room. I walked over to the bed, while Jake hung back a little. Ray looked troubled, but when he saw that I was there, his mood lightened instantly. "Suzanne. You came."

"Just like Jake did. You ask, and we appear," I said. There was a bandage on the back of his head and an IV tube in his arm. From the whiskers on his cheeks, he hadn't shaved in a few days, and there were dark circles under his eyes, showing that he'd had a rough time of it lately.

Still, he was better off than Tom Thorndike.

"I appreciate that, from both of you." Ray looked past me and spied my husband. "Jake, would you give us a minute?"

"I'm working for you on this, remember?" Jake reminded him.

"I haven't forgotten," he said, and then a whisper of a smile appeared. "If only I could say that about everything else. Please?"

Jake nodded. "I'll be right outside if you need me."

"Were you talking to me or Ray?" I asked him.

"Both, I guess." My husband was clearly unhappy about being excluded from the conversation, and I wasn't quite sure why Ray was sending him away, but I wasn't about to insist that Jake stay with us.

Once he was gone, I asked, "So, why all the mystery, Ray?"

"Suzanne, did we speak last night? I mean this morning? At the donut shop when you got there?"

"No, of course not. Why do you ask?"

Ray shook his head. "I had the oddest feeling that we had, that I was at the donut shop last night, and we talked for a few minutes before you started working. Are you sure?"

"Ray, given all that's happened, it's not likely that I'd forget something like that," I said.

"Maybe you wouldn't, but I clearly did." He reached up a hand and touched the bandage on his head lightly. "I've still got a headache, even with the meds I'm on, and my mind is just a jumbled mess."

"Do they know what happened?"

"Apparently I hit my head on a rock, but that's all anyone is willing to admit," he explained. "I don't remember any of it. Funny, but I'm usually pretty sure-footed. I can't imagine tripping and falling, but that's the doctor's best guess."

"Ray, were you at Laurel Falls yesterday evening just before dark?"

He frowned. "Not that I recall. I can't imagine going up there on my own. I don't know if you know this about me, but I'm not a big fan of heights."

"I didn't know that, or if I had, I must have forgotten it." I needed to stop saying that. Every time I used the word "forgot," it seemed to act as some kind of trigger for Ray, not that I could blame him. If I'd had a chunk carved out of my recent memory, I'd probably be sensitive about it as well. "Ray, do you remember writing this?" I reached into my back pocket and pulled out my folded copy of his note to Tom. The moment Jake had told me that I was being summoned to Ray's bedside, I knew that I needed to bring it with me.

The newspaperman glanced at it, and then he nodded. "Yes. I remember leaving it. I'd uncovered something about Tom's recent past, and I wanted to ask him about it. He wouldn't see me, though I suspected he was inside the cottage while I pounded away on the front door. I scrawled a quick note on my card and slid it under his door, but it didn't do any good. He tore it up and threw it away, didn't he?"

"I found it in the trashcan," I admitted. "Do you happen to remember what you discovered?"

"I wish I could, but it's all still a blank. It's odd. Things seem to come and go even past the sixteen hours I lost completely. One second I'll have it, and the next it will be gone."

"Ray, do you keep notes on your stories?" I asked him.

"I do," he admitted. "They're gone. Jake looked for me, but he couldn't find them among my things. Suzanne, if I was working on a story, I would have had a notebook on me, guaranteed."

Something about that sent a chill through me. "What do you suppose happened to it? Do you think someone might have taken it?"

"I don't know. For all I know, I might have hidden it myself."

"Why would you do that?" I asked him.

"Clearly I found something that I didn't want anyone else to know about." He paused, took a sip of ice water, and then added, "Including me."

"Where should I look for it?" I asked him. I'd already told

him that I hadn't seen him the night before, and he'd just about lost interest in talking to me as soon as I'd told him that I hadn't seen him. That didn't mean that I was finished with him yet, though. "Could it be in your office?"

"I have no memory of it, but if you want to have a look around, there's a key on top of the gutter downspout near the back door. I keep it there for emergencies."

"You'd really be okay with me taking a look?" I asked him.

"You'd be doing me a favor," he said. "The sooner I get my memory back, the better."

I had another copy of something in my pocket, one of the button and shirt fragment I'd found on the trail. "Does this look familiar?"

He studied it for a second, and then he handed it back to me. "No, should it?"

"Probably not."

"Where did you find it?"

I hesitated telling him, and then I realized that it wouldn't do any harm. "It was on the trail to the falls, and it looked as though it had just been torn off someone's shirt. Don't worry. Jake's already checked your clothes. It wasn't from anything you were wearing."

"Let me see it again," Tom said, reaching for the color copy. After I handed it to him, he looked at it again. "I've seen this shirt before. As a matter of fact, I think it used to be mine."

"Used to be?" I asked him.

"I donated it to the thrift store six months ago. What does it mean?"

"I'm not sure yet. You're certain you donated it?"

"Right now I could barely swear to my name. Ask Sharon. She'll know for sure."

"Okay. Listen, I'm sorry that I couldn't help," I said. "You were smart to get Jake to help you piece your memory back together. If anyone can help you do it, it's my husband."

"I hope he has better luck than he has so far," Ray said. He must have been feeling better, because there was a hint of acid in his voice as he said it. If he'd been truly hurting, I suspected that he would have been nicer.

There was a knock at the door, and Sharon came back in carrying a tray. "Dear, you've got to try this. It's wondrous."

"What is it?" he asked. "Is it okay with the doctor?"

"He thought it might do you some good," Sharon said, and then she turned to me. "Are you two finished here?"

"For now," I said. "Feel better, Ray."

"Thanks for coming, Suzanne."

"I'm just sorry I couldn't help."

"You tried. That's all you can do."

Then I remembered the image of the shirt fragment. "Sharon, does this ring any bells with you?"

She took one look at the copy and then handed it back to me. "It used to belong to Ray, but I donated it to the thrift store, along with a dozen other shirts I couldn't stand. Why? Is it important?"

"It could be," I said. "I don't know yet. You're certain?"

"Positive. That shirt has been out of my house for a good six months. I remember, because I purged his closet right before our anniversary." She looked back at her husband. "Remember?"

"I'm not about to forget the Great Closet Purging," he said with a smile for his wife.

So, it had once belonged to Ray, but now who knew who had it? It might mean something, but then again, it might be just another false clue sending me galloping off in the wrong direction.

Only time would tell, and I felt as though that was one commodity I was quickly running out of.

CHAPTER 18

J AKE WAS WAITING FOR ME when I walked out. "Anything?"

"No, it's all still a big blank. He's feeling better, though."

"How could you tell?"

"He got snippy with me that you couldn't find more than you have," I said with a grin.

"Yeah, that sounds about right. He's not completely wrong. Ray doesn't exactly dance through life in the shadows. You'd have thought that *someone* had seen him."

"Don't worry. You'll figure it out."

"I hope so."

"There's one more thing. He recognized the shirt and button fragment."

"It wasn't from his clothes," Jake said. "I'm sure of it."

"Sharon confirms that he donated it to the thrift store six months ago, so anybody could have it now."

"Anybody that shops at the thrift store," he said.

"Is it a coincidence, or is it a real clue?" I asked him.

"I have no idea at this point. Are you ready to go home?"

"After we pick up our order," I told him with a smile. "You don't mind eating leftovers for the next few days, do you? I'm not thrilled about freezing such a masterpiece."

"I was about to suggest the same thing. I don't think I could ever get tired of that cooking." He paused before adding, "Not that your meals aren't great, too."

"Spare me," I said with a laugh. "I'd rather eat his food, too."

I suddenly realized that in all of the commotion, I'd forgotten to tell Jake about the pictures on Tom's camera. But first I needed to tell him that Ray had given us permission to search his newspaper office.

When I told him the news, he seemed surprised. "Did you get the key somehow? I asked him about it earlier, but he said that he'd lost his wallet and keys, including the ones to his office and his home."

"He has a spare. Did he not tell you about that?" I asked.

"No, but to be fair, he was still pretty fuzzy the last time we spoke. I'm guessing that his mind is finally clearing up."

"Maybe so. Do you feel like going over there with me? After we drop these packages off at home first, that is. I know it's chilly out, but I don't want to take any chances. I want these containers safe in our fridge."

"Yes, that would be great."

Was there a hint of hesitation in his voice as he said it? "You don't mind if I go with you to the newspaper office, do you? I know Ray's disappearance is your case, but if we can find his notes on Tom Thorndike, it might help me out as well."

"Sure. That makes sense." If my husband was unhappy about me going with him, he wasn't going to tell me. Ordinarily I would have declined to go with him if I thought it might not please him, but this was too important. Something in Ray's notes might reveal what had really happened to Tom, and I couldn't afford to miss the chance to find out one way or the other.

After dropping the food in our fridge back home, Jake and I headed straight for the newspaper office. I'd been there before, but it was never a space I was all that comfortable in. I hated clutter as a general rule, but I doubted that Ray Blake could think straight without it. We parked and got out, and I found the key, just as promised.

Instead of opening the door myself though, I handed it to Jake and said, "Be my guest."

"Suzanne, I don't have to be the first one inside."

"Nonsense. It's your investigation. I just appreciate you letting me tag along with you."

Jake grinned at me, and I suddenly felt better about everything. "We both know that you don't tag along anywhere. If I'm not quick enough getting through the door, I have a feeling I'm going to get run over."

"Then be quick, and we won't have to find out," I said with a laugh.

The newspaper office hadn't changed much since I'd been there last. It was always in such a messy state that if someone ransacked the place as they had done in Tom's cottage, I wasn't sure I'd be able to tell. Besides stacks of old newspapers, there were reference books on just about everything scattered throughout the space. Had Ray never heard of the Internet? The office was a fire hazard, and I was relieved to see water sprinklers featured prominently overhead. Ray had a small personal office off to one side, and it was no better than the rest of the place.

As Jake and I walked through the open door, he whistled softly to himself. "How can anyone work in all of this chaos?"

"I know I couldn't do it," I said as I approached his large desk. "Is this a door?" I asked as I knocked on the wood. Sure enough, Ray hadn't spent any money on a conventional desk. Instead, two small file cabinets served as a support for a door salvaged from somewhere else on the property. "You know what? This is actually kind of handy."

"Cheap, too," Jake said. Besides the litter on the desk and all around on the floor, even the walls were covered with notes. At some point Ray had taken insulating board and had it installed on two of his walls. Pinned to this shiny foil-covered board were notes on stories he was working on, at least so I presumed.

The mayor appeared to be one of his favorite topics: several handwritten notes featured George Morris prominently. What did he have against my friend? Maybe it was simply the fact that he was mayor, but I didn't like some of the notes he'd made.

"Did the mayor buy his own truck, or did someone give it to him as a bribe? Is he hiding money in one of those foreign accounts I keep hearing about? When he was a cop, was he ever accused of police brutality? Dig into this!"

The notes offended me to the core, and I hoped that George never had cause to read any of them. Anyone who saw the mayor's truck would never suspect that it could have been a bribe. As to having money in foreign bank accounts, I couldn't imagine the man's net worth reaching five figures. The brutality question struck me as being particularly harsh. I had faith in George's character, and I couldn't even fathom the possibility that he'd ever used undue force on someone. "Can you believe all of this?"

Jake read the notes, and then he shrugged. "Honestly, I'm not all that surprised."

I looked hard at my husband, since he was friends with the mayor as well. "Doesn't this make you angry?"

"Suzanne, I've heard worse things about me that news people have said directly to my face. It's part of the world George lives in. The higher you are on the ladder, the clearer shot your critics have at you."

"Wow, I'm glad I'm just a donutmaker."

"You, my love, are anything but just a donutmaker," he said with a slight smile.

"Thank you, but it still makes me angry."

"I can't do anything about that," he said as he started pawing through the stacks on Ray's desk. "If there's a clue hidden somewhere here, I can't imagine where it's hiding."

"This is hopeless, isn't it?" I asked, agreeing with him.

"I wouldn't say that. It's just going to take some grunt work."

"Why doesn't that fact discourage you as much as it does me?" I asked as I picked up a stack at random. According to the top sheet, it appeared that Ray had been looking into the possibility that a mysterious millionaire was buying up property in April Springs for nefarious purposes. As I scanned the list of places recently purchased written in bold, I recognized some of them. My mother was our own answer to a land baron in our part of the world. I didn't have an inkling as to the vast expanse of her holdings, but I had a hunch that she'd been involved in at least some of the transactions that had clearly alarmed Ray. Momma liked to treat properties in town as though they were part of some complex game of Monopoly. Did Ray honestly believe that her motives were sinister? If he did, I hoped that he never found out the true extent of her holdings.

"It's kind of what I've always done," Jake said. "A large part of being a good cop is being stubborn and never giving up, no matter what the odds."

"It's an admirable trait, just one that I've never developed myself."

"I'm afraid we're in for a long night," Jake said. "If you need to go home and get some sleep before your early morning starts tomorrow, I don't mind wading into this alone."

"Thanks for the offer, but I think I'll hang around a little while longer," I said. I stood there with my back against the door, and on a whim, I started swinging it back and forth. As I moved it, I noticed that something had been attached to the side that would close off the room from the outside. Swinging the door fully closed, I found myself suddenly staring at a whiteboard filled with notes about Tom Thorndike!

"Will you look at that," Jake said as he took in what I'd just found. "Good work, Suzanne."

"Don't give me too much credit," I said as I studied the scrawls written on it. "It was sheer dumb luck that I even found it at all."

"That's another part of police work most cops don't like to talk about," he said with a grin. "Let's see if we can make any sense of it."

The whiteboard was three feet by five feet, and someone had permanently screwed it to the door. In the center was a small circle with spokes radiating from it in a dozen different directions, but scrawled in the middle of it was the name T. Thorndike.

As I started following different paths, Jake asked, "Would you mind stepping back for a second? I want to get a photo of this."

That was a great idea. I took a few shots myself, enlarging the shot until I could get all of the board in focus. After we finished, I asked, "Any idea about how we should tackle this?"

"Carefully," Jake said as we both approached it again. "This spoke has Mitchell Bloom's name on the line. Below that, with what I'm assuming are Ray's theories, is that Tom and Mitchell committed some kind of crime together." After a moment's pause, he tapped the board with his index finger. "What does that say?" Jake asked as he squinted at the board. "Does it say, '*he's it*'?"

"I think it's supposed to be one word, '*heist*'," I said. "Was there a heist around here that I don't know about?"

"Nothing comes to mind, but we'll keep it under consideration," Jake said. "Here's one with George's name on it. Why am I not surprised?"

It immediately raised my blood pressure knowing that the newspaperman was trying to rope the mayor in on yet another wild theory of his. "What does it say?"

Jake squinted, and then he read, "It appears to claim that Tom got his money by blackmailing the mayor about something in his past."

"Where is George supposed to have gotten all this money in the first place?" I asked.

"You don't want to know," Jake said, trying to shield me from the board.

"Don't be silly. I can just check the photo on my phone if you won't tell me," I told my husband. He stepped aside, and I saw that Ray had scrawled, "*Is he rich from being on the take as a cop?*"

"Are you kidding me?" I asked indignantly.

"Suzanne, it's not that unusual for a cop to be accused of it at one time or another in his career."

"Someone accused you of taking money?" I asked him.

"More than once," Jake said with a smile.

"What's so funny about that? I fail to see anything amusing about it at all."

"I always took it as a compliment, myself," Jake answered.

"I don't see how."

"I figured that if they started going after me personally, it usually meant that I was on the right trail." Jake tapped another spoke. "This one just says '*stranger*,' and there are a series of question marks around it. Do you know any strangers that should be on this list?"

I suddenly remembered the conversation I'd had outside my donut shop earlier. "Just one that I can think of offhand."

He looked at me oddly. "Go on. You've certainly managed to get my full attention."

"I didn't mean to keep anything from you, Jake. There's just been so much going on that I haven't had a chance to tell you. Somebody offered to buy my donut shop today."

My husband shook his head in disbelief. "And this is how you choose to tell me?"

"It wasn't a serious offer," I said. "What he really wanted was an excuse to ask me about Tom Thorndike."

"How can you be so sure?"

"Trust me, if he were serious, I would have known it."

"You didn't happen to catch his name, did you?"

"Daryl Lane," I said promptly.

"Okay. We need to run a check on him and see what his story is," Jake said as he reached for his phone. "Only I can't really ask the police chief, since he still doesn't think Tom was murdered. I don't get why he's so set on thinking it was an accident."

I put my hand on my husband's to stop him from calling whoever he'd been about to contact. "There are a few things that I should probably mention before you talk to him."

Jake's lips turned into two thin lines for a moment, and then they relaxed. "Suzanne, how is it that you're making more progress than I've been able to so far?"

"I found this out from Grace," I admitted. "Apparently Tom was quite the daredevil, taking photos of himself in some pretty risky situations. The last shot on the phone was of him with his back facing the waterfall. The chief believes that the fall was from him being careless, not because he was murdered."

Jake nodded and got really quiet for a few moments. I knew better than to disturb his train of thought. After a full minute, he said, "That makes sense, then."

"Do you believe that it was an accident now?"

"I still don't know, and neither can Stephen," Jake said. "We both need to keep digging. You said there were two things."

"Oh, it's about Daryl Lane. The chief looked him up on some kind of criminal database, and he told us that the man was in prison at the same time Tom was. Not only that, but evidently he's a very bad guy indeed."

Jake shook his head. "So naturally he's in town right around the time Tom died. If he's not tied into this mess somehow, I'll be surprised. But we can't do anything about him; he's the police chief's problem. All we can do is keep digging on our end."

"I wasn't about to stop," I said, remembering the promise I'd made George. "I wish we had a timeline for all of this."

"It would be nice, wouldn't it?" he asked me as he continued to stare at the board. "This is all well and good, but where is Ray's actual notebook? I've never seen a reporter without one, and Ray would have a set of notes on hand wherever he went to refer to if he needed to. I went through his belongings after I agreed to look into his absent memory, remember? There were no notes, no pads, nothing; the man didn't even have a pen on him."

"Isn't that unusual in and of itself?" I asked him.

"Absolutely. He's a newspaperman, and what's more, he's clearly not a fan of technology. He should have had that notebook, or something like it, on him. So the real question is, where is it now? Whoever has that notebook might have had something to do with all this, 'maybe' being the operative word."

I followed another spoke on the board and found Candy Murphy's name included. Below it was a simple question: "*Girlfriend? Maybe more, or maybe not at all.*" "What do you suppose he meant by that?"

"I'm guessing that he saw them together, but he wasn't sure how she fit in."

"To be fair, neither am I," I said. It was getting hot in the office with the door closed. "Are we finished with this for now? It's really stuffy in here."

"Sure. Should we open the outside door and let some fresh air in?"

"That's a great idea," I said as I opened the office door and moved out to the front.

I was about to grab the handle when I saw it begin to turn of its own accord.

Apparently someone was trying to get into the newspaper office.

CHAPTER 19

"Quiet," Jake whispered to me as he moved beside the door.

"What are you going to do?" I asked him, keeping my voice low as well.

"I'm going to see who's trying to get in."

I watched as he grabbed the doorknob and jerked it open.

George Morris nearly fell on the floor of the newspaper office when he did.

"George, what are you doing?" Jake asked him as he steadied the man, keeping him from falling.

"I noticed that there was a light on in here, and I wanted to check it out," the mayor replied. "I heard that Ray was going to be held in the hospital overnight for observation, so I knew nobody should be in here. You two didn't break in, did you?" he asked us with a grin.

"As a matter of fact, Ray told us where he hid a key," I said. "Mr. Mayor, how do you two get along?"

"I thought everyone in town knew. He thinks I'm the devil himself," George said, his smile never fading. As he looked around the space, he said, "I can't imagine the kinds of things he's got written down about me around here."

"Trust me, you don't want to know," I said, trying to block his way. I knew the mayor was a tough old bird, but that was still no reason to put the burden of the newspaperman's suspicions onto him.

"You know what? I find that I really do," he said. "You don't mind if I look around, do you, Jake?"

My husband turned to me. "He at least has the right to know what he's up against, Suzanne."

I could see Jake's point, but I still wasn't sure it was a good idea. "Are you positive, George?"

"Now I really want to see," he said. "I suspect you two have already found several references to me by the way you're acting. What does he say? Was I responsible for the global banking meltdown, or perhaps he believes I was on the grassy knoll in Dallas. Do you want to give me a guided tour of the man's delusions, or do I have to root them out for myself?"

"Come on," I said. After George saw the things we'd found regarding Ray's general suspicions, we led him into the man's office and closed the door to let him study the whiteboard we'd found.

George whistled softly as he studied the branch with his name on it. "Wow. Just wow."

"Consider it a compliment," Jake said. "He's certainly got a target painted on your back, doesn't he? There's a great deal of wild speculation there, and no evidence whatsoever to back any of it up. You seem to be his favorite hobgoblin, but if it's any consolation, I'm sure that whoever was in the mayor's office would get the same amount of random speculation shot in their direction. After all, it's the highest-profile office in April Springs. You were a cop, so Ray wonders about graft and police brutality. If you were a lawyer, he would have accused you of fabricating evidence, and if you'd been a businessman, he would have accused you of having connections to organized crime."

George shrugged. "At least he never printed any of this nonsense. I take some consolation in the fact that I never touched a single suspect, nor did I take a dime from anyone, not even a cup of coffee on the house."

"I can attest to that," I said, trying to lighten the mood. "You won't even accept a free donut from me, and we all know how delicious they are."

George stared at the board for another few seconds, and then he turned away. "He might actually have Tom's killer on that board."

"George, I'm not positive he was murdered," Jake said softly. The mayor looked at him sternly. "What makes you say that?"

Jake told him about the photos that had been found on Tom Thorndike's cell phone, and George slumped a little. "He told me that he hated being locked up so much that when he got out, he'd explore the world and follow wherever his heart led him. Tom told me the riskiest thing anyone could ever do was to let a moment slip through their fingers, not doing something when they had the opportunity. I've thought a lot about what he told me, and I've come to believe that he was right. I know that he had darkness in him that he constantly struggled with, but deep down in his core, he was a good man."

"Does that mean that you believe it was an accident now?" Jake asked him.

Instead of answering my husband's question, the mayor turned to me. "Is that what you think, Suzanne?"

"I honestly don't know," I told him. "I have to admit that it's a possibility, but I still believe it's also within the realm of reason that someone pushed him off the edge of that waterfall. If you want me to drop it, though, I will. I'll do whatever you say."

He nodded, and after a few moments of silence, he said solemnly, "Give it one more day, would you? If, by this time tomorrow, you're convinced that it was an accident, I'll go along with you on it." The mayor turned to Jake. "You and Stephen think that's exactly what it was, don't you?"

"Barring the appearance of evidence leading us to believe someone had a hand in it, I'd feel safe saying that, yes. I'm sorry."

"Sorry? I'm not," George said with a hint of lightness in his voice. "I hope with all of my heart that you're right. Much better an accident than murder." The mayor glanced back at me as he added, "One more day of digging, Suzanne, unless you're out of leads."

"No, I've got a few more things I want to check out," I said. "Grace has been a big help, and so has Jake."

"I would expect nothing less from either one of them," he said with a sigh. "Now, if you'll excuse me, being around all of this rampant speculation about my character and potential sins is giving me a headache. Good night."

"Good night, Mr. Mayor," I said as Jake echoed the sentiment.

Once the mayor was gone, Jake looked at me. "This has really weighed heavily on his heart, hasn't it?"

"He bonded with Tom after he arrested him," I explained. "Did anything like that ever happen to you?"

"No, but then again, I usually went after a substantially worse brand of criminal than he did. Suzanne, this place is depressing me. Let's get out of here."

"Sounds good to me. We've got an hour before bedtime. Is there anything else you want to check out before we head home?"

"Not me. How about you?"

"The only thing I want to do right now is to go back to the cottage, change into my jammies, build a fire, and dive into a good book. I've got a new cozy mystery I need to finish before the book club meets again next week."

Jake grinned at me. "Where do I fit into those plans?"

I winked as I told him, "You can sit and read one of your true crime books beside me on the couch, if you're good."

"Then I really hope that I'm very, very good," Jake replied.

We did exactly that, and I left him reading as I crept off to bed an hour after we arrived home. I had to get up in seven hours and make donuts yet again for the world of April Springs.

And if I was lucky, I might be able to solve a murder, too.

I'd been at the donut shop all of six minutes when I heard someone pounding on the front door. I considered ignoring it, but then I realized that it might have something to do with my investigation into Tom's death, so I grabbed my trusty baseball bat and flipped on the outside lights as I walked from the kitchen to the dining area.

It was Barton, the chef from the hospital we'd met the night before. "Hi! I didn't think I'd see you this soon," I said as I unlocked the door and stepped aside to let him in.

"Getting in a little batting practice, Suzanne?" he asked me with a grin. "I hope I'm not disturbing you."

"As a matter of fact, I'd like the company," I said as I put the bat on the counter. "What can I say? A girl can't be too sure these days."

"I don't blame you a bit." He looked outside for a moment. "Everything looks so different in the dark, doesn't it?"

"It's one of the things I love best about my job," I said. "Come on back, Chef."

"You can call me Barton," he said with a grin. "I'm still getting used to the whole chef thing. Besides, if you insist on calling me that, then that's what I'm going to call you. I've tasted your treats, remember?"

"Barton it is," I said. "Let's go make some cake donuts."

"Lead the way," he said.

I grabbed a spare apron and handed it to him, as well as a hairnet. He put them both on with a smile and rubbed his hands together when he saw my ancient equipment. "Does this fryer even still work?"

"Like a charm," I said, feeling a little defensive about my less-than-pristine tools. "Sometimes the oldies are goodies."

"I couldn't agree with you more," he said as he spied my donut cutters tucked under one cabinet. "These are awesome. Did they come with the business?"

"Some of them. I've been picking them up as I find them," I admitted. The aluminum cutting wheels, outfitted with maplewood handles, were some of the favorite things I owned, and that included every bit of jewelry I had besides my second wedding ring. The one Max had given me was in the bottom of some drawer at home, but I wore Jake's proudly every day of my life.

"These are beautiful. You don't roll out the cake donuts, do you? Do you drop them by hand, or do you have a dropper?"

"I use this," I said as I handed him the heavy-duty donut dropper. The cake batter was loaded into the reservoir on top and then forced by gravity through the narrow tip into the hot oil.

"I wouldn't want to arm wrestle you," he said with a grin. "This thing is massive."

"You should see what happens when it slips out of my hands," I replied, smiling. The young man's mood was infectious, and I grinned as I showed him the divot in the wall where I'd inadvertently let go of it once. "When I drop donuts, I have to do it alone, unless you want to take the risk of being hit by this thing flying through the air at you."

"I'll take my chances. I've survived worst situations," he said happily.

"Then on your head it will be."

"Are we still making Kool-Aid donuts this morning?" he asked eagerly.

"We are," I said. As I gathered the ingredients, we chatted about recipes and how we each kept notebooks filled with information not only about what we made but what we dreamed about at night. I'd never really had that kind of bonding experience with anyone else, and though our lives and our training had been completely different, there was enough common ground for an instant friendship to develop between us. I hated the thought of Barton moving so soon after meeting him, and I decided to tell him so. "I can't believe you're leaving us so soon. I have a feeling that you and I have been friends who just hadn't met yet, or do I sound crazy?"

"If you do, you're my kind of crazy," he replied. "The truth of the matter is that I've been having second thoughts about leaving. April Springs is a quaint little place, and I'm not thrilled about relocating to the big city. I just don't have a good enough reason not to go, I guess."

"I understand being young and wanting to get out and see the world," I said. "My assistant, Emma, feels the same way."

"I've seen her around town. She's really pretty, isn't she?" he asked shyly.

"She is indeed, but there's a great deal more to her than that. Emma is smart, funny, and loyal to a fault. I count myself lucky to have her in my life."

Barton held his hands up in surrender in front of him. "Hey, I wasn't saying that she was *just* a pretty face. All I said was that I thought she was cute."

"Sorry," I said, letting my intensity fade. "I'm kind of overprotective of her."

"I can see that. It's just a shame she isn't here. I wouldn't mind meeting her."

"That might be arranged," I said, deciding at the last second not to tell him that she'd be in shortly. "Now, let's mix this batter up and start frying."

"After we do these, I'd love to see your pumpkin donut recipe. That's all some folks in town are talking about, how happy they are that they're back on the menu now that cool weather is back."

"Sure. Why not? Just promise me one thing," I said in all seriousness.

"What's that?" Barton asked, sensing the somber tone of my mood.

"Don't start serving homemade donuts at the cafeteria while you're here," I said. "I wouldn't be happy if you took my recipes and used them against me."

"I would never do that, Suzanne. You have my chef's oath," he said, laying his hand on his heart. "I promise that I won't do anything to violate the trust you've placed in me."

True to his word, Barton stayed in the kitchen as I dropped the batter rounds into the fryer, and I was happy that he was uninjured in the process. After I glazed a few of the bright Kool-Aid donuts, I offered him one on a plate.

He took in the aroma then tried a tentative bite. The smile that bloomed on his face was enough to make an old donutmaker feel as though she weren't wasting her life making treats for other people. "Do you really like it that much?"

"So much so that I'm going to steal it, with your permission. I'm thinking about using this as a base for one of my cakes, though I'll have to fiddle with it, of course, to get the portions just so."

"For that, you have my blessing," I said with a laugh.

Barton finished the last bite, and after he reluctantly declined when I offered him another, he asked, "Okay, now we've done the pumpkin donuts and the Kool-Aid ones, too. What's next? I heard that your orange-glaze cake donut is wonderful. Do you happen to have the ingredients for that batter on hand, or am I being too demanding? If I'm pushing you too much, just say the word and I'll tone it down a bit."

"You're just fine," I said. I'd been planning on doing some orange-zest cake donuts sometime during the week, so fortunately I had all of the supplies I needed in my kitchen already. "Let's get started," I suggested as I pulled out my recipe book and began gathering ingredients. Many of my cake donuts started out with the same basic recipe, and each variation was merely a case of additions, but it certainly wasn't true across the board.

We'd finished making most of the more exotic cake donuts I offered my customers at Donut Hearts when Emma came through the kitchen door. "Suzanne, are you okay? I could swear that I heard voices..." she said, her words trailing off when she spotted the fact that I wasn't alone.

"Emma Blake, this is Barton..." I stopped and looked at him. "I just realized something. I don't know your last name."

"It's Gleason," he said as he held out his hand to Emma. "It's a pleasure to meet you, Emma. According to Suzanne, you're someone worth getting to know, something I don't doubt for a single second."

Emma actually blushed as he took her hand, but she quickly found her poise again. "Don't believe everything you hear. Suzanne has a tendency to exaggerate."

"If anything, I undersold you," I said with a grin. "Why don't you two go out front and get acquainted? I've got to get the yeast dough together."

I could tell that Barton was torn between his thirst for knowledge and his desire to get to know my assistant, so I made the decision for him. "Barton, I've truly enjoyed having you in the kitchen with me, but I need to focus, if you don't mind."

It was one of the bigger lies I'd ever told in my life, but he seemed to buy it. I could mix the dough for my yeast donuts in my sleep; it was the cake ones that offered so many variations. "Emma, there's coffee ready out front. Why don't you treat our guest to some?"

"Sure thing," she said. "This way," Emma told him as she pointed to the door.

Once he was through, Emma shot me a curious but definitely intrigued look. I just grinned, shrugged, and then shooed her away.

Maybe, if things worked out, Barton would find a reason to stay after all, but if he didn't, it wouldn't be from my lack of trying. I wasn't sure that Jake would approve of my matchmaking, but I was happy being in love, so why shouldn't the rest of the world be able to experience it as well? Emma wasn't the world's best judge of good boyfriend material, so maybe she needed a little nudge in the right direction, just as her friend Jennifer had.

In my defense, I hadn't planned on anything happening between them, but once Barton had mentioned her to me, the wheels hadn't been able to stop turning.

I'd done all that I could, though.

Now it was up to the two of them.

CHAPTER 20

I STAYED IN THE KITCHEN AS long as I could, but I knew that if I didn't go out front soon, I'd miss my break outside, and that was something I cherished more than young love, especially this time of year. October was hands down my favorite month, with chilly temperatures, moons so big they almost looked surreal, hot chocolate, and pumpkin donuts—pumpkin donuts most of all. There was something about the flavor that I adored more and more every year, and I was constantly trying to incorporate it into my autumn offerings.

I frowned for a moment when I realized that the front was empty when I walked out, and then I saw Emma sitting by herself at our outside table where we usually took our breaks year-round, no matter what the weather might be.

"What happened to Barton?" I asked as I joined her, pulling my coat close to me.

"He had to go get some sleep before his shift starts," Emma said. "That was really smooth, Suzanne. Are you trying to fix us up?"

"I resent that remark," I said with a smile.

"Resemble it, you meant to say. There, I fixed it for you," she added with a grin of her own.

"He wanted to see me make Kool-Aid donuts," I said. "That led to pumpkin, and then to orange zest."

"You showed him our greatest hits? You really must like him."

"What can I say? He strikes me as a good guy, Emma, and there aren't enough of them around to suit my taste."

"I get it," she said. "It's just that he's leaving town, so there's not much of a future for us, is there?" The last bit she added a little wistfully, and I knew that she longed for a relationship with someone she could count on. She'd dated more than her share of duds over the years, but I had to give her credit; she always thought the next one would be different.

"I'm sorry you two won't be able to go out," I said.

"I didn't say that," Emma replied as she looked at me and smiled. "As a matter of fact, we're going out on a date tonight."

"That's great," I said, trying to contain my enthusiasm. If Barton gave Emma any kind of chance, I had a hunch that he might just find the reason he'd been looking for to stay in April Springs.

"Now, enough about my love life," she said. "It was sweet of you to come by the hospital last night to see Dad."

"I'm just sorry that I couldn't help. How's he feeling?"

"Cranky and ready to leave the hospital, which I take as an excellent sign." She frowned a moment before adding, "I just wish he could remember the parts that he's still missing."

"It's eating him up, isn't it?"

"Suzanne, he's afraid that he might have had something to do with Tom's fall," she confessed to me.

"Why would he think that? It's not as though he and Tom had an argument about anything before it happened."

Emma looked as though she wanted to cry. "That's the thing. He's starting to remember bits and pieces, and one of them is him confronting Tom about his past and his shady present."

"Where did this happen?" I asked, trying to hide my yearning to know.

"It's foggy, but he thinks it was outside. Whether it was at Laurel Falls or not, he can't say. Suzanne, I know you aren't my dad's biggest fan, but on his worst day he'd never kill someone. I refuse to believe it's even a possibility."

I understood why she felt that way, but I imagined there were a great many killers out there whose children weren't able to accept the facts. "I understand," I said.

"Do you honestly believe that he could have done it?" she asked pitifully.

"Certainly not on purpose," I answered carefully. "Accidents do happen, though."

"Like Tom falling off the edge taking a picture of himself," she said. "Chief Grant came by after you and Jake left and told us why he believes it was an accident. Dad was a little guarded when he heard the news, but Mom believes it vindicates him completely."

"Why shouldn't she?"

"You still think it was intentional, don't you?"

I had to be careful how I answered her, but my assistant deserved the truth. "George still isn't convinced, so I'm going to keep digging until he tells me otherwise."

"Why is the mayor so involved?"

"They were friends," I said simply, not wanting to get into their past relationship. There was no reason to dredge it all up with Emma.

"It's an odd pairing, isn't it? Dad has some kind of compulsion to believe the worst of our mayor. Did you know about that?"

"We were in his office, remember? Before you get too upset with me, he gave us his blessing. What we found seemed a little far from reality." It was the nicest way I could think of to tell her that I thought her father was crazy.

She seemed to take it in stride. "Dad does that sometimes. He likes to think up these outrageous scenarios, and then he tries to prove or disprove them. He says it's what separates him from other newspapermen."

I didn't doubt it, but not for the reasons he believed it proved. "Okay."

"I don't believe the mayor did it any more than I think my father had anything to do with what happened to Tom Thorndike. Who does that leave, though?"

"Are you asking me as a friend or your father's daughter?" We'd butted heads in the past over times that Emma had crossed the line, and I wanted to make sure it never happened again if I could help it.

"You're right. Sorry. Forget I even asked," she said good-naturedly as my timer went off. "Time to make the donuts," she said as she stood.

I joined her and gave her a quick hug. "I'm glad your dad is doing better."

"Thanks. I really appreciate it."

The rest of the prep work went smoothly, and I was glad to have Emma back in the kitchen with me. I'd missed her the day before, and I decided to tell her just that. "I've got to say, it's a lot nicer here with you than without you," I said with a smile.

"I hate that I dumped all of those dishes on you," she said.

"It was okay. Momma came by and helped out."

"You're kidding, right?" she asked in amazement.

"No, I'm not. Why does that strike you as odd?"

"I don't know. Your mother is such a prominent woman in town, I have trouble imagining her up to her elbows in sudsy water."

"She's a lot more down to earth than you might imagine."

"I'll take your word for it," Emma said as she continued washing.

"It's time to open our doors to the public," I told her three minutes before six. "Are we set out front?"

"The display cases are full, the coffee and cocoa are finished, the chairs are down, and the cash register is loaded, so as far as I'm concerned, we're ready," Emma said with a smile.

"What are you doing here?" I asked Daryl Lane an hour after we opened. "I know you aren't interested in buying the donut shop. It's about Tom Thorndike, isn't it?"

"I don't know what you're talking about," he said calmly. "I came by for a fritter."

"Sorry, but we're all out," I said.

He pointed to the case behind me. "Really? I can see five of them right there."

"They've already been sold. I'm holding them for another customer," I lied.

"He can manage with four."

I could see the darkness in him when he said it. "Fine." I grabbed a fritter and shoved it into a bag. I quoted him the price, and he shoved a five-dollar bill toward me. After handing him his change, I smiled my brightest, most insincere smile and then said, "Have a nice day," in a way that said, "Go away and never come back."

"Oh, I will," he said, and then he took his fritter to a table, removed it from the bag, and started eating it right there in my shop. I slipped into the kitchen for a second as I pulled out my cell phone.

"He's here," I said as soon as the police chief answered.

"I'll be there in five minutes. Can you stall him without putting yourself in danger?"

"I think so, but hurry."

Emma looked at me oddly, but I just shook my head and

went back out front. Pouring a cup of coffee, I also grabbed another fritter and headed to Daryl's table. As I put them both down in front of him, I said, "I want to apologize for before. I'm having a bad day, but that didn't give me any right to take it out on you. These are on the house."

"I thought these were for someone else," he said, ignoring my offering.

"I can always make more."

"Okay," he said, and when I continued to stand there, he looked up at me and said, "You can leave now."

I turned and went back to the front counter, trying my best to hold in my temper. I had never been dismissed like that in my own shop, and it didn't sit well with me, but I was doing this for the police chief, so I decided that I could swallow a little pride in the process and just let it go.

It was just too bad that my ploy didn't work.

He dropped the fritter he'd bought onto the bag, took one bite of the one I'd given him, ignored the coffee completely, and then left the entire mess on the table for me to clean up.

In a moment he was heading for the door, and I needed to delay him if I could.

"Was there something wrong with the fritters?" I asked him.

"They were bland, dry, and overcooked," he said. That got the attention of several of my customers, who seemed to collectively hold their breaths waiting for my explosion.

They weren't going to get it, at least today.

"I'm so very sorry for the inconvenience," I said. "I'd be happy to give you something else, or would you rather have a full refund?"

"Forget it," he said as he headed out the door.

I had tried my best to stop him, but since that hadn't worked, I needed to see where he was going so I could tell the chief where to start looking.

I followed him outside, and Daryl Lane took three steps away from the donut shop before he whirled around and faced me. "Is there something I can do for you, Suzanne?"

"I just wanted to get a little fresh air," I said, uncomfortable with his proximity.

"Get it somewhere else," he growled. As he started to storm off, I took my last shot at delaying him.

"Why are you so interested in Tom Thorndike, anyway?"

Daryl stopped dead in his tracks, pivoted, and got within an inch of my face. "Mind your own business, lady."

"Hey, you came into my shop, remember?"

"Yeah, that was a mistake, wasn't it? If you have something to say to me, then say it. Otherwise, you need to steer clear of me. Do you understand?" He'd said it with an icy quality to his voice that chilled me to my core.

"Or else?" I asked, trying to show him that I wasn't afraid of him, which would have been quite an accomplishment, since at the moment, I was terrified.

"Or else you'll live to regret it," he said. "Do we understand each other?"

"Loud and clear," I said with relief as the chief pulled up in his squad car, followed closely by another cruiser. He had brought reinforcements, and I didn't blame him a bit.

"Daryl Lane?" Chief Grant asked as he got out of his car.

Instead of answering, the stranger stared hard at me for a few seconds, and then he said, "You set me up."

"I don't know what you're talking about," I said. My voice didn't shake nearly as much as it should have.

"You're going to be sorry you did that," he said as Chief Grant tapped him on the shoulder. "What can I do for you, Sheriff?" he asked, his tone shifting to a nicer level than I'd ever heard from him.

"It's Chief," Stephen Grant said. "I'd like to have a word with you."

"About?"

"About an hour, if everything goes smoothly, but that's entirely up to you. Why don't you get in my car and I'll give you a ride to the station?"

It was clear Daryl had taken that particular ride before. "No, thanks."

"I'm sorry. Were you under the impression that you had an option?" There was steel in the chief's voice, and I saw that the man was growing into his job quite nicely after all.

"Fine," Daryl replied. As he got into the front of the car, he stopped to look back at me. "I'll see you soon, Suzanne." There was more of a threat than a promise in his voice, and I found myself troubled by this man's attention. This was a focus I didn't want on me, and I had no trouble imagining him pushing Tom Thorndike off the edge of the falls.

"I'm not going anywhere," I told him, never breaking eye contact. I'd been nervous before. Now I was just plain angry.

The ex-con seemed surprised by the resolve in my voice, and he looked away before I did.

I was still staring at him as the chief drove off, and I saw Daryl glance back at me once before they turned off Springs Road toward the station. I'd have to be a little more careful until this thing was resolved, but I wasn't about to let one man stop me from doing what I'd set out to do.

CHAPTER 21

"I'M GUESSING NOBODY'S BUYING DONUTS for the house today, are they?" Seth Lancaster asked as he ordered three pumpkin donuts and a pumpkin-flavored coffee. I was afraid he might overdose on the flavor, but I filled his order anyway.

"No, everyone pays for their own today," I said with a smile as I made change from his twenty.

"In a way, that was my money Mitchell was using, anyway," Seth said.

"What do you mean by that?"

"I was one of the big losers in the poker game where he won it," Seth said. "That should teach me to gamble. Maybe I'll stick to the lottery. I've had more luck with scratch-off tickets anyway."

Seth suddenly had my interest. Mitchell had claimed to win the money playing poker, but I'd questioned it. Had he been telling the truth after all? "You were in that game?"

"You heard about it? Yeah, I was there, along with Mitchell, Tom Thorndike, Jeff Granger, and a few other guys from Union Square. Mitchell was the big winner, and Tom lost the most, even more than I did. He didn't have enough to make his final bet, and Mitchell let him put an IOU in the pot. He lost it, and I thought Mitchell was going to explode when Tom said he wasn't going to pay up."

"Is that what they were arguing about in the park a few nights ago?" I asked, ignoring the three folks waiting in line to get their donuts. They'd just have to be patient. This was important.

"Yeah, Mitchell told me about that. Tom finally paid up, and to show him that there were no hard feelings, he brought Tom by the bar and bought him a drink. I was there too, and you'd never know there had ever been any bad blood between them. By the time they left, they were best friends, and a day later, poor old Tom was dead. You just never know, do you?"

"Suzanne, I'm in a bit of a hurry," Lilly Hamilton said from the back of the line.

"Sorry, I didn't mean to hold you up," Seth said. "I love this time of year. Pumpkin rules!"

"I'm glad you like them," I said absently. As I waited on the next customer in line, I realized that one of my suspects had just been cleared. It appeared that Mitchell Bloom had won his money fair and square after all, and after Tom had paid off his debt, the two men had parted friends. Unless I learned something to the contrary, Mitchell's name needed to go off my list. I had never considered the mayor a suspect, and Ray had always been a stretch for me as well. George had been the reason I was investigating Tom's death at all, an unlikely scenario if he'd actually killed the man, and Ray, though he had his faults, wasn't a murderer, at least not for as thin a motive as he might have had. Besides, if he'd done it, Jake would uncover it, not me. I had too much faith in my husband to believe he wouldn't eventually uncover the truth about the newspaperman.

Daryl Lane was a very possible candidate, given his police record as well as his contacts with Tom, but he was the police chief's problem for now.

That left me with Candy. Could the gym owner have pushed Tom over the edge? I'd seen her muscled shape in those skimpy outfits, so I knew that she was strong enough to do it. But that still left me with the question of why. Was there more to the note we'd found at Tom's, or was it as simple as she'd explained to us? I wasn't sure, but I knew that I wasn't finished with her quite yet, and I wouldn't be until I got the answer to that, unless Jake or the police chief managed to solve the case before I could.

A little before ten, my husband came by the donut shop, but he clearly wasn't there on a social call. "Hey, Suzanne. Do you have any coffee?"

"Pumpkin spice, or our regular blend?" I asked him as I grabbed a cup.

"Just plain old coffee," he said. "It's getting so you can't find it anymore."

"Emma likes to play with our coffee offerings," I said as I poured Jake a cup of our regular brew. "Sometimes I wonder about her choices, but the pumpkin spice seems to be popular. This time of year, it's tough to get *anything* without pumpkin in it."

"I know. We've got that cereal in our cabinet, don't we?" he asked, and then he took a healthy sip of coffee. "That's tasty. Any chance I could get an old-fashioned donut to go with it?"

"Are you sure you wouldn't like pumpkin instead?" I asked him with a grin.

"No, and no Kool-Aid donuts, either. Just the usual, if you don't mind."

"I'm happy to give you whatever you want, but you can't blame a gal for trying. What brings you by, not that you need an excuse to come by Donut Hearts anytime I'm here?"

"I got a call a few minutes ago that's been bothering me," he admitted. I put his donut down on the bar by the counter so we could chat and I could still wait on any customers who might come in. Fortunately, we were experiencing a lull at the moment, but I knew that could change at the drop of a hat, so I wanted to be close to the register, just in case.

"Who called you?" I asked as I poured myself a little hot chocolate, just to be social. That wasn't entirely true; I loved the stuff, much more than I liked coffee. My drinks, in order of preference, usually went: sweet tea, water, hot chocolate, chocolate milk, plain milk, and then coffee. I'd never been that big a fan of sodas, though I'd been known to have one now and then.

"Some woman. She wouldn't leave her name, but she told me that she heard I was looking into Ray's disappearance, and she said that she had something I needed to hear."

"That sounds ominous. Any idea what she was talking about?"

"No, and when I pressed her, she said that she'd only do it face to face. I'm meeting her at noon in Union Square in front of Napoli's."

Napoli's was an Italian restaurant run by our friends, Angelica DeAngelis and her lovely daughters. "You're going to have lunch there first, aren't you?" I asked him.

He grinned at me. "Well, since I'm already going to be in town during lunch hour, I thought I might go a little early so I could grab something. It would be rude not to."

I laughed. "I'm not sure that it would be rude, but I do think passing up a chance to go there would be foolish."

"Come with me," Jake said. "You can close the shop a little early, and we can make it a date."

"I'd love to, but I hate leaving everything to Emma. Can I have a rain check?"

"Of course you can. I'll tell Angelica and the girls you said hello."

"You do that," I said with a smile. I knew that it wouldn't be that much of a hardship for him to be waited on by the group of beautiful women. He usually didn't enjoy getting attention, but

I had a hunch he'd make an exception in this case. "You're going to be careful, aren't you?"

"I promise I won't eat anything that's too spicy," he said.

"That's not what I meant, and you know it. It sounds as though it might be a trap."

Jake shrugged. "At this point, I'd take it. I'm beginning to think that Ray slipped, knocked himself out, woke up with a headache and no memory, and then started wandering around town until someone found him."

"What about Tom?"

Jake took a bite of donut, smiled briefly, and then said, "It could all just be a coincidence."

"You hate coincidences, and you know it," I reminded him.

"True enough, but they still happen sometimes."

"If you really believed that, you wouldn't go to this meeting," I said.

"Maybe not. Anyway, I just thought I'd stop by and let you know what's going on. How's your morning been?"

"Well, besides being threatened by a convicted felon, it's been pretty quiet," I said softly.

"What? What happened?"

I told him about my exchange with Daryl Lane, and he got angrier by the minute. "Suzanne, what were you thinking going after him like that?"

"Jake, the police chief asked me to stall him. Nothing happened, so there's no reason to get upset about it after the fact."

"Grant should have never put you in that position," Jake said a little sullenly.

"He didn't. In fact, he told me *not* to confront him. It was my decision, so if you're going to get mad at anybody, it should be me." I loved the fact that my husband was so caring, but sometimes he acted as though I hadn't been able to manage on my own before he came along. If I had to, I'd remind him of it now and then, though. "So, are you going to accept the fact that I did what I thought was right, or are we going to argue about it?"

It appeared to be touch and go for a second before he shrugged. "Sorry. I know you can take care of yourself, but this is a bad guy we're talking about. I can't help worrying about you."

I touched his hand lightly. "I love you for it, but I saw something that needed to be done, and I did it. You would have done the same thing, and you don't have any more authority than I do."

"Maybe not, but I've handled this type before."

"I'm not exactly a rookie at it, either," I said with a smile. "More coffee?"

"No, I've got some other leads to follow up on before I go to Union Square. If you change your mind, give me a call."

"I probably won't, but thanks for thinking of me," I said as I leaned across the counter and kissed his cheek. "Be careful, okay?"

"Right back at you," he said with a smile. "It's okay for me to say at least that much, isn't it?"

"If you ever stop worrying about me, that's when we're going to have a problem," I answered him happily.

"Then we'll be good for a very long time," Jake said. He polished off his donut, drank the last of his coffee, and then he stood. "I'm assuming you don't want me to pay, right?"

"You could, but it would be kind of pointless, since it would just go back into the family bank account."

"I know, but I still like to ask."

After he was gone, I considered cancelling my sleuthing plans for the afternoon, closing up early, and going with Jake to Napoli's after all, but I decided that we could always go there after the mystery surrounding Tom Thorndike's death was resolved one way or the other.

In the meantime, I had donuts to sell.

CHAPTER 22

HALF AN HOUR BEFORE CLOSING, I got a phone call as I was cleaning up a mess left by three toddlers and a very frustrated babysitter. I didn't know how much she made an hour, but in my opinion, it wasn't nearly enough.

"Hello?"

"Suzanne, it's Chief Grant."

"Chief. What's up? You haven't let Daryl Lane go already, have you?" I had a sudden image of the man storming toward my donut shop even as we spoke, and I even moved to the front so I could look out the window and see if he was coming. He was nowhere in sight, but that didn't necessarily mean that he wasn't on his way.

"No, he's not going anywhere for quite a while. Right now he's cooling his jets in one of my jail cells."

"You arrested him for murdering Tom?" I asked. Was it possible the man had confessed to the crime I was still trying to solve?

"No, he denies ever being up on Laurel Falls, but it wouldn't surprise me if he had a hand in it as well."

"What do you mean, as well?" I asked him.

"Well, when I implied that we were looking at him for murder, he suddenly got pretty talkative. It's amazing what a man will tell you when he's trying to save his own skin."

"What did he say?" I asked as I made change for a customer as I cradled my phone between my cheek and my shoulder.

"It turns out that he was in Tom's cottage when you and George showed up," he said. "He didn't mind giving that up, since he assumed he'd been spotted running out the back. He said that he figured that was why you were so intent on bracing him at the donut shop this morning."

"I had no idea that he'd been there, and neither did George," I confessed.

"You know what they say, 'The wicked flee when no man pursues.' He figured he'd cop to that much, at least."

"Why was he there?" I ask. "Was it about Tom's money?"

"You've been busy, haven't you?" the chief asked me. "That's exactly what he was doing. He tracked Tom down when he got out of prison to settle an old score, but when he found out Tom had money, he shifted his focus from revenge to robbery."

"He killed Tom for the money?" I asked softly. It always amazed me what some people would do for little pieces of paper that intrinsically were worthless but represented untold greed to so many.

"He claims he never found it. As a matter of fact, he didn't get into town until after Tom died. He went to South Carolina to ask one of Tom's old cellmates if he knew about the money. We spoke to the man, and apparently Daryl was there when Tom died."

"Where did the money come from? Did he say?"

The police chief was in a talkative mood, and I wasn't about to discourage it, even if it meant that my customers didn't get my full attention.

"Believe it or not, he robbed a check-cashing business as soon as he got out. Tom gave the old con some money he'd owed him when they'd been inside, and he told him the whole story while he was there."

George had hoped that Tom had reformed, but apparently it had only served to make him a better robber than he'd been when he'd gone in. I knew the news would disappoint my friend, but I couldn't worry about that at the moment. "So that explains that. Did you arrest him for breaking and entering? Is that why he's locked up?"

"No, he earned that particular privilege by taking a swing at me," the chief said.

"Did he hurt you, Stephen?" I asked, reverting to calling my old friend by his first name when I realized that he could have been injured in the line of duty.

"He tried to, but he must have slipped and hit his head on the table. He'll be fine, but I have a feeling he's going to have a headache for quite some time. Anyway, I just wanted to touch base with you and let you know what I'd found."

"I appreciate that," I said.

"Suzanne, I still think you're chasing shadows."

"I get it, but until George calls me off, I'm going to keep at it."

"I would expect nothing less from you," the chief said with a chuckle. "Well, I'm going to let Mr. Lane have some time to reflect on the choices he's made in his life, and I'm going to take a little break. I'll talk to you later."

"Thanks, Chief."

"You're very welcome," he said, and then we ended the call.

I began to wonder if it were possible that Tom really had slipped from the top of the falls. I'd liked Daryl Lane for it, but he had an alibi, and Mitchell Bloom was in the clear as well. Unless either Ray or George had undergone a major personality change without me realizing it, that left just Candy on my list of suspects, and again, why would she do it? I'd probably go talk to her with Grace after work just to wrap things up in my mind, but essentially, my investigation was nearly over. I wasn't exactly torn up about the resolution, and not because Tom had reverted to a life of crime once he'd been released from prison.

We make our own choices in this life, and it's not up to any of the rest of us to judge them, good or bad. I had enough trouble being responsible for my own actions, let alone worrying about someone else's. That didn't mean that I approved of what he'd done. Wrong was wrong. But however it had happened, Tom was finished with the temptations and tribulations of this world.

As I waited on another customer, I couldn't help thinking about how sometimes one bad choice in life was all it took to send someone on a path they couldn't, or more likely wouldn't, break free of.

As I prepped to close for the day, even though we still had twenty minutes on the clock and there were a few customers lingering over their coffees and donuts, I decided to give Grace a call to see if she'd like to join me when I closed the shop and paid a visit to Candy Murphy.

"Hey," I said. "How's the paperwork going?" I asked her when she answered the phone.

"I'm taking a little break," she said, and I could hear road noises in the background. "Hang on a second. Let me roll up my window. It's so pretty out that I decided a little fresh air might be in order."

"Will you be long? I'd love to do a little more detecting as soon as I close the shop for the day."

"Sure. I'll call you. Suzanne, I can't really talk. I'll talk to you later."

She hung up on me before I had a chance to even reply. What was she up to? It wasn't like Grace to cut our conversations off so abruptly. If I didn't know any better, I might believe that she was up to something. But what? Oh, no. What if she'd come to the same conclusions I had about Candy being our last viable suspect, and she hadn't been able to wait for me before she confronted her? I wouldn't put it out of the realm of possibility. Grace had been known to be rash in the past.

I called her back immediately, but she didn't answer her phone.

I was really getting worried now.

Fifteen minutes before I was due to close, I decided that I couldn't take it anymore.

"Emma, we're shutting down early," I said as I went back into the kitchen.

"Are we out of donuts already?" she asked me happily.

"No, but I've got something I need to take care of, and it can't wait."

"Suzanne, just go. I can handle things here on my own."

That particular thought hadn't even occurred to me, even though she ran the shop with her mom two days a week without me. "Are you sure?"

"You've covered enough times for me in the past," she said. "Go."

I didn't need any more incentive to take off. "Thanks. I owe you one."

"Let's just say that I owe you one less of the ten thousand times you've done something sweet for me," she said happily.

As soon as I had her settled up front, I took off my apron, grabbed my jacket, and headed for Grace's. It was so close that it made sense to try there first. Maybe it was all in my imagination, and the reason she hadn't picked up was because she was already busily back into her paperwork.

The only problem was that her company car wasn't there.

That left Candy's gym. Maybe she was staking the place out, waiting and watching until I could join her.

So why hadn't she picked up her phone?

I was nearly at Candy's gym when my cell phone rang.

It was Grace, and I suddenly felt relief wash over me.

Then I heard who was on the other end of the line.

"Suzanne, your friend has been a very bad girl. Unless you meet me at the top of Laurel Falls in fifteen minutes, she's going to meet the same fate as Tom Thorndike did, and you don't want that, do you?"

"Don't hurt her, Candy," I said, feeling my face go numb.

"I won't do a thing, unless you disobey me. Don't call anyone, don't bring anyone with you, and don't try anything funny. If you do, she's going to die. I can promise you that much." From the background, I heard Grace shout, "Don't do it, Suzanne!"

I had started to protest when Candy hung up on me. At least I knew that Grace was still alive; for how long, I didn't know.

I thought about calling Jake, Chief Grant, or even the mayor, but the idea quickly died in my mind. If I did that, and something happened to Grace because I'd disobeyed Candy's orders, I'd never be able to forgive myself. She'd sounded so chillingly rational when she'd given me my orders that I was afraid to do anything other than what she'd just told me to do. I didn't have a weapon in the Jeep, just a tire iron, but if I came up that path with a weapon of any sort, I had a hunch that Grace wouldn't have long to live. There was no way to sneak around and surprise Candy, either. That path was narrow and more than a little bit steep, hemmed in on one side by woods and on the other by the waterfall itself.

I was just going to have to wing it and hope for the best if I had any chance to save my best friend.

CHAPTER 23

A s I came up the last part of the path, Candy yelled from above me, "That's far enough, Suzanne. Empty your pockets, and take off that jacket. I want to see you throw your cell phone over the edge before you do another thing, or Grace is going to die."

I didn't do anything yet, though. "Grace? Are you okay?"

"She can't answer you. After that last little outburst, I had to gag her, but don't worry, she's just fine. At least for the moment."

I wasn't sure if I believed her or not, but I didn't really have any choice. I took out my cell phone and did as she'd instructed, tossing it into the waterfall and watching it disappear.

"Very good," Candy shouted, as though I'd just passed the first of a series of tasks for her. The waterfall was loud here, but I could still hear her. "Now the jacket and your pockets."

I was suddenly glad that I hadn't brought the tire iron with me. As I did as I was told, I asked loudly, "Why did you grab Grace?"

"The fool followed me up the path. I lost a button and part of my shirt somewhere, and I came back to hunt for it."

I realized that the button and cloth had come from Candy and not one of our male suspects. Too late I remembered the work shirt she'd been wearing when we'd talked to her at her gym. Though it was a different material, it was clear that Candy favored those types of shirts. "You get your shirts at the thrift store, don't you?"

"Very good. I find them nicely broken in by then. You've been busy, haven't you?"

I'd made a serious mistake; there was no denying it. I just hoped that my slip didn't end up costing Grace and me both our lives.

Candy went on, "When I realized someone was following me, I hid behind a tree until she caught up with me. I called you while I still had a signal on her phone, and then I smashed it on a rock. Nobody's with you, are they?"

"No, I came alone, as instructed," I said. "Can I at least see her?"

"Come on up, but keep your hands in the air," she commanded loudly.

I did as I was told, and when I reached the clearing, I saw that Candy was holding Grace near the edge of the falls where Tom had gone over. It was even louder up there at the moment, but I had to do something to distract her, or Grace was going to die. I was strong enough to run my donut shop, but Candy owned a gym, and she clearly worked as a trainer there as well. Strong and evil was a combination I didn't really want to mess with, but I didn't have much choice.

"What's your plan now?" I asked her loudly over the sound of the water.

"Do I look like someone who has a plan?" she asked me, and for the first time, I saw a little of the crazy in her eyes that she'd been so good at hiding.

"Before you do anything that can't be undone, wouldn't you at least like *someone* to know how smart you've been? If you get rid of us now, nobody will ever know." I was playing on her ego, and I hoped that as she spoke, Grace or I could come up with something that might save us both.

"Why not? Everybody always thought I was some pretty little idiot. They had no idea I was playing them, including Tom."

"Why did you kill him? What did he ever do to you? It was about that note we found, wasn't it?"

Candy frowned. "He kept asking me out, that much was true, and I kept saying no. He tried to impress me with his money, and he flashed a bunch of cash around. Tom knew that my gym was in trouble, and he tried to use the money to get me to do things with him that I was never going to do. Don't ask me what they were. I don't want to talk about that." She looked clearly troubled by the memory, and I didn't want her any more upset than she already was. When I didn't say a word and instead did my best to look sympathetic, she continued, "I pretended to be interested in him, and once I got him back to his place, I gave him some knockout drops. I searched that pigsty top to bottom, and I finally found his money. He was furious when he woke up! I told him that I'd give it back to him at the top of the falls, and that I'd taken it to teach him a lesson. The fool believed me! I didn't trust him, though, so I waited beside the path to be sure he was alone. After he passed me by, that moron Ray Blake came up the path right behind him! He was going to ruin everything, so I hit him on the back of the head with a rock. All I can say is that man must have a thick skull. I figured he was dead. Imagine my surprise when he showed up the next day. Anyway, he wasn't going to give me any more trouble at the moment. It took me a few minutes to deal with him, and when I got to the top, that lunatic Tom was taking a photo of himself at the falls. It was almost too easy with all the noise to sneak up on him and give him a little shove."

"So you had no intention of ever giving him his money back," I said.

"His money? His?" she shouted. "He stole it, and I took it from him. I needed that cash. He was just wasting it!"

"Did you take Ray's notebook after you knocked him out?"

"You caught that, did you? Yes, when I thought I'd killed him, I figured I'd plant it on Tom's body later. Murder/suicide, you know? Only before I could do that, I heard someone at the base of the falls, so I threw the notebook into the woods. As far as I know, it's still in there somewhere."

"You're not going to get away with this, Candy. I told the police where I was going and who I was meeting up here. Do you think the chief is going to rest one second until he catches you? Or my husband? You might as well give up right now. It's over. Jake and Stephen will find you and make you pay for what you've done." It was all pure bluff, but I didn't have any other option at that point.

"Do you honestly think they're going to be good enough to catch me once I disappear for good?" she asked, though she was clearly troubled by me bringing logic into it.

"You'd better believe it," I said. Grace made a gesture with her eyes, and I realized that she'd come up with a play. Her eyes shot straight down a few times, and I finally got it. She was going to throw herself down away from the falls, and I needed to do something to force Candy over the edge. I didn't even hesitate, though I had no desire to push this woman to her death. In the end, if I had to choose between Candy's life and ours, I would choose us every time.

It sounded like the best plan we could come up with given so little time.

Neither one of us could be blamed for the fact that it didn't work out that way.

CHAPTER 24

GRACE WENT DOWN INTO THE water, and I tried to lunge at Candy. At least that much went according to our hasty plan. The main problem was that Grace only managed to partially free herself from Candy's grip, pulling her down to the busy water along with her. The two of them were in danger of going over the edge, so I did the only thing I could think of.

I grabbed them both.

There was a moment when Candy had to release her grip on Grace in order to stand up, so I took the chance to pull Grace up and out of the water.

Candy slipped on a rock as we climbed out.

It was just the bit of luck we needed, but would it be enough?

"Run!" I shouted at Grace as I led her back down the path. There was no sense in trying to fight Candy, not even accepting the fact that it was two against one. We weren't used to fighting, and I'd seen kickboxing bags at Candy's gym. In a fair fight, I had a feeling that we'd be easily subdued.

So I wouldn't play fair.

As we stumbled toward the path going downhill, I glanced back and saw that Candy had quickly recovered her balance and was after us. Was it wrong that I'd hoped she'd slip over the falls and share the same fate Tom had? No matter; it wasn't going to happen.

As we started down the steep path, I knew that if we stayed

on the trail, Candy would quickly overtake us. The only chance we had was to branch off into the dense woods. I pulled Grace off the path. She was gagged and her hands were tied, so she couldn't say anything, but I could see in her eyes that she was as terrified as I was.

As we disappeared into the dense forest, I could hear Candy gaining on us. Glancing back, I nearly missed a dramatic drop in the layout of the land. A tree had been pushed over in a heavy storm years before, and it had left a large hole with moss-covered rocks beneath it. I would have tumbled into it if it hadn't been for Grace pulling me back just in time. Could we use it to our advantage? There was a heavy branch lying to one side of us that had broken off from above. I grabbed it without thinking and urged Grace to go on, skirt around the hole, and act as bait on the other side of it.

Maybe, just maybe, I'd be able to catch Candy off guard at just the right time.

It was the only chance we had left. Either it worked, or I had a feeling that neither Grace nor I would live another day.

CHAPTER 25

GRACE STUMBLED AS SHE NEARED the other side of the hole, and she went down in a heap. Had it been planned, or was she really hurt? I couldn't afford to check on her, at least not yet. I had to deal with Candy one way or the other and hope that Grace was okay.

"There you are," Candy said as she nearly tumbled over the edge that had nearly caught me. She looked insanely happy about finding Grace, and she must have forgotten about me for an instant.

That was what I'd been counting on.

Stepping out from behind a tree, I swung the branch with everything I had, aiming for her head.

She saw it in time and somehow managed to grab the limb out of my hands.

My plan had failed completely.

CHAPTER 26

"YOU'RE GOING TO PAY FOR that," Candy said as she looked down at me. When she'd intercepted the branch meant for her head, I'd lost my balance, and I'd slipped on the damp leaves. The sun didn't reach that deep into the canopy, and I wondered if they'd ever find our bodies if she took the slightest care in hiding them.

I was trying to scramble up to my knees when Candy lifted the branch high above her head, and I prepared myself for the impact of her blow.

But it wasn't just slippery under me.

Somehow the momentum of lifting the branch caused Candy to lose her footing, and I saw the instant of panic in her eyes as she fell over backward into the hole that I'd planned to send her into in the first place.

There was a dull thunk as she hit, and I scrambled to look over the edge to see what had happened.

"My leg is broken," she said in a cry. "Get down here and help me, Suzanne."

Had the woman completely lost her mind, demanding my aid after trying to kill me and my friend both? "Sorry. I have something else I need to take care of first," I said as I hurried toward Grace, who was on her feet now. The fall had been a feint after all, and I felt relief flood through me. "Are you okay?"

She'd pulled the gag away, though her hands were still bound. As I untied her, she asked, "Is she dead?"

"No, she just broke a leg," I said happily.

"Help me," Candy screamed.

Grace laughed, more from relief from humor. She called out, "We'll go get someone. Now don't you go anywhere, you hear?"

The language coming out of that hole was enough to burn the bark off the trees around us, and I was a little surprised that her temper didn't set the whole forest on fire.

CHAPTER 27

THE NEXT DAY, THINGS WERE back to normal at the donut shop, or at least as normal as they could be. Emma came in grinning, and I had a hunch what had caused it. "How did your date go last night?" I asked her as she put on her apron.

"Barton's decided to stay," she said with a smile.

"Wow, that was quick," I said.

"It's not *all* because of me, Suzanne. He told me that he was having second thoughts before he met me. I'm just the icing on the cake, so to speak."

"How does that make you feel?" I asked her, doing my best not to smile, just in case she'd been offended by the comment.

"I don't know about you, but there are times for me when the icing is the best part. Anyway, we're going to take it slow, but I'm really happy he's staying."

"So am I," I said. "He's a good guy. How's your dad doing?"

"He's upset, if you can believe that," Emma said.

"Because you're dating a chef?" I asked.

"He could care less about that. The biggest story to hit April Springs in years, and he missed it! I think he's relieved to know what happened and that he wasn't responsible for Tom Thorndike's death, but he couldn't even run a special edition."

"I wouldn't worry about that if I were you. I'm sure that he'll find a way to write a firsthand account of this. You just wait and see," I said, not entirely unkindly.

"I'm sure you're right. Can you believe what Candy Murphy did for money?"

"I've seen enough over the past few years to believe anything when it comes to greed," I said. "I'm just sorry that Tom had to pay for it. Once upon a time, he was a good guy. It just goes to show you what your choices can do to you."

Emma nodded. "If you'll drop those cake donuts, I'll get started on setting up in front. Then I can tackle the dishes."

"Sounds good to me," I said.

We'd been open a few hours when Jennifer, Emma's jilted friend from the park, came in holding hands with a boy who looked as happy as anyone I'd ever seen before in my life. Before they ordered, she said, "Suzanne, do you know Lee?"

"Hey, Lee. How's it going?" I asked, feeling the contagious nature of their happiness.

"Couldn't be better, ma'am."

I could have done without being called ma'am, but he was a polite young man, so I decided not to hold it against him. After they got their donuts, I cleaned up a little. It felt good working in my shop again and getting back to normal. I'd seen yet again what greed and the unending pursuit of money could do to people, and I was just glad that I hadn't been bitten by that particular bug myself. I had more than enough to be happy. Who needed anything more than that? I was rich in many ways, just not my bank account. Having money wasn't necessarily bad. My mother was one of the richest people I knew, but she never let it control her life. She'd taught me well as a child, and I was happy to have had the lessons. I was certain she'd be amazed to realize just how much she'd showed me, mostly by example, and I meant to share it with her as soon as she got back from her trip.

In the meantime, I had a lunch date with my husband in Union Square as soon as Donut Hearts shut down for the day.

His description of his meal at Napoli's had made me decide that I couldn't wait another day for Angelica's wondrous offerings.

And we had plenty of money to cover our bill, with a nice tip to boot.

Beyond that, what more did we really need, in the scheme of things?

RECIPES

I N THE SPIRIT OF FULL disclosure, if these recipes seem familiar to you, it's most likely because they were either taken directly from past books or modified slightly before they were added here. I've decided that in order to offer more mysteries to you, my dear and valued readers, I'm going to take a break from creating new recipes in my kitchen for a bit. For every recipe I've shared over the past twenty-five Donut books (not to mention the Cast Iron and the Classic Diner mysteries), there were usually at least five that didn't make the cut, so when writing a novel that offers three recipes, it normally means that fifteen to twenty are required. The first ten books featured at least ten recipes each, so that means that I, and my tasters, decided that at least fifty weren't good enough to share, though they achieved various degrees of tastiness among us. Over the course of these books, I've pretty much depleted my recipe idea notebook, and I haven't been able to keep up with the demand for new ones, so at least for now, I'm going to offer some of my old favorites, including these. If you didn't have a chance to try one of these in the past, now's as good a time as any, no matter what season it might be when you're reading this. As I write this note of explanation to you, it's September in the South, and we're finally beginning to believe that autumn is in the air after a long, hot, dry summer. This time of year inspires some of our favorite recipes, and I hope you enjoy them as much as my family and I do!

Kool-Aid Cake Bites

When I heard about these donuts being served at our county fair, I had to try to come up with my own recipe, adapting them to donuts. The taste, as well as the color, is BOLD! We love these, so if you're feeling adventurous one day, try them!

Ingredients

Mixed

- 1 egg, lightly beaten
- 3⁄4 cup milk
- 3⁄4 cup sugar, white granulated
- 2 tablespoons butter, melted
- 1 teaspoon vanilla extract

Sifted

- 2 cups flour, unbleached all-purpose
- 1 full packet of powdered unsweetened Kool-Aid mix, .13 oz. (we like Tropical Punch!)
- 1 tablespoon baking powder
- Dash of salt
- Canola oil for frying (the amount depends on your pot or fryer)

Directions

In one bowl, beat the egg lightly, and then add the sugar, butter, and vanilla. In a separate bowl, sift together the flour, Kool-Aid packet, baking powder, and salt.

Add the dry ingredients to the wet, mixing well until you have a smooth consistency. It's fun to do this one with your kids, because when you mix the dry and wet together, the colors go from bland to BRIGHT!

Drop bits of dough using a small-sized cookie scoop (the size of your thumb, approximately). Fry in hot canola oil (360 to 370 degrees F) 1 1/2 to 2 minutes, turning halfway through.

Yield: 10–12 donut holes

Orange Zest Donuts

I got this idea from some treats my mother-in-law used to make at Christmas. They featured the candied oranges cut into cubes and added to an applesauce cake recipe. She baked hers in loaves, and we started making them in cupcake tins when I realized they would make a great baked donut! Making these adds a rich cinnamon taste to the air, and they are worth trying for that alone!

Ingredients

Wet

- 1 1/2 cups milk (2% or whole)
- 1 cup granulated sugar
- 1/2 stick butter (1/4 cup), melted
- 3 egg yolks, beaten
- 2 tablespoons canola oil
- 1 tablespoon orange extract
- zest of one orange, finely grated

Dry

- 1/4 cup orange slice candies, cubed
- 1 teaspoon cinnamon
- 1 tablespoon baking powder
- 3-4 cups flour

Directions

In a large mixing bowl, stir in the milk, sugar, melted butter, beaten egg yolks, canola oil, orange extract, and orange zest thoroughly until everything is well combined. In another bowl, stir together the cubed candy pieces, cinnamon, baking powder, and 3 cups of flour. After slowly adding the liquid, stir the mixture well. This will make a nice batter, but feel free to add more flour or milk to the mix in order to get a batter that easily scoops out on the edge of a tablespoon.

Place in donut molds, or scoop out tablespoon-sized balls on a cookie sheet and bake at 375 degrees F for six to eight minutes, or until they are golden brown and spring back to the touch.

Yield: 8–10 Dunkers

Pumpkin Donuts

We love these donuts around Thanksgiving and make them quite often when there's frost or snow on the ground. The flavors are subtle, but the pumpkin taste is there, and it makes a nice change of pace from the usual donut.

Ingredients

- 2 eggs, beaten
- 1 cup sugar
- 2 tablespoons canola oil
- 1 can pumpkin puree (16 oz.)
- 2/3 cup buttermilk
- 4–5 cups bread flour
- 1 teaspoon salt
- 4 teaspoons baking powder
- 1/2 teaspoon baking soda
- 1 teaspoon nutmeg
- 1 teaspoon cinnamon
- 1/2 teaspoon ground ginger

Directions

Beat the eggs well, then add the sugar, mixing until it's all incorporated. Add the oil, pumpkin, and buttermilk, then mix that all in. In a separate bowl, combine all of the dry ingredients, holding back 1 cup of the flour, using 4 cups of flour, the baking powder, baking soda, salt, nutmeg, cinnamon, and ground ginger. Sift the dry ingredients together and add them slowly to the egg mixture. Once you've got them well mixed, chill the dough for about an hour.

Once the dough is thoroughly chilled, roll the dough out on a floured surface until it's about 1/4 inch thick, then cut out donuts and holes with your donut cutter. While the donuts are resting, heat the oil in your fryer to 375 degrees. Add the donuts to the oil a few at a time, turning them once after a couple of minutes. Take them out, drain them on a rack, then they're ready to eat. These are good with powdered sugar on top, or just plain.

Makes approximately 1 dozen donuts.

If you enjoy Jessica Beck Mysteries and you would like to be notified when the next book is being released, please send your email address to **newreleases@jessicabeckmysteries.net**. Your email address will not be shared, sold, bartered, traded, broadcast, or disclosed in any way. There will be no spam from us, just a friendly reminder when the latest book is being released.

Also, be sure to visit our website at jessicabeckmysteries.net for valuable information about Jessica's books.

OTHER BOOKS BY JESSICA BECK

The Cast Iron Cooking Mysteries
Cast Iron Will
Cast Iron Conviction
Cast Iron Alibi
Cast Iron Motive

57176887R00109